PRAISE FOR MISTLETOE & MISSING PERSONS:

MISTLETOE AND MISSING PERSONS

A Mariposa Café Holiday Mystery

by

Teresa Michael

First Electronic Edition: November 2019
First Print Edition: December 2019

eBook and Print Book design & formatting by
D. D. Scott's LetLoveGlow Author Services

To My Mom,
Grace Costello
Who always made sure we
Had a family Christmas Eve

Table of Contents

Chapter 1

Mid-November, Late afternoon, Mariposa Beach, Florida
There's a New Guy in Town

When Libby Marshall stepped out of the bank on Mariposa Boulevard, an open door in the shop across the street caught her eye. She had just dropped off the deposit from the Mariposa Café, which she ran with her business partner, Mimi, when she noticed the door to the boarded up shop was wide open.

Eleanor's Gifts was sandwiched between The Village Dress Shoppe and The Surf Shop in a typical, small town city block of three conjoined buildings with storefronts on the first floor and apartments upstairs. The shop had been shuttered since the previous February. The eclectic gift shop had been a staple in Mariposa Beach for about forty years until Eleanor, at almost seventy years old, suffered a stroke standing at the cash register while ringing up purchases for Canadian visitors. Within a few days, Eleanor passed away, and her shop was boarded up. The furniture and shop inventory as well as the contents of her upstairs apartment were as she had left them, as if waiting for her return.

Libby glanced toward the café on the next block, and then to the beach two blocks beyond. The café was not busy mid-afternoon, and Mimi wouldn't expect her back too soon on such a beautiful autumn day. Libby was known to occasionally take the scenic route back to the café after making the bank deposit.

She checked for traffic before jogging across the street. She stopped on the sidewalk and peeked in the open door. The boarded up windows and yellowish glow of the table lamps created eerie shadows that bounced off the china animals, crystal vases, and carnival masks. The interior of the shop was the same as the day Eleanor was wheeled out on the gurney, albeit quite a bit dustier.

A tall, fair-haired man that Libby estimated to be in his early to mid-thirties was standing in the middle of the cluttered, dusty shop with a well-dressed, shorter Asian man.

"Hello," Libby said.

The men turned. "Hello," the tall man said with a smile.

"I'm Libby Marshall from the Mariposa Café down the street. I couldn't help but notice the open door."

"I'm Steve Devereaux," he said with a soft Southern drawl.

Steve was wearing dusty cargo shorts, a faded T-shirt and a dark baseball cap.

"This is Kenji," he said, pointing to the shorter man who wore a form-fitting, black T-shirt and tan trousers. He fingered a short gold chain necklace as he nodded a greeting.

"Sorry for intruding, but the door was open, and my curiosity got the best of me."

"We're cleaning out the building in preparation for some renovations," Steve said.

"I'm so glad someone bought this building," Libby said. "The whole block looks depressed with this shop all boarded up."

"It was my Aunt Eleanor's shop," he said. "I decided to buy out my relatives, renovate the building and open a photography studio and art gallery."

"Did you decide on a name for the gallery?" Kenji asked.

"I'm thinking about calling it The Devereaux Gallery. What do you think?" he asked. "I have a couple of other ideas, but I keep coming back to that one."

"I like it," Libby said. "It's classy."

"It works," Kenji said. With his left hand on his hip and his right hand outstretched to the room, he asked, "What are you going to do with all this...this stuff?"

"She had so much inventory," Libby said. "There's knick-knacks, candles and figurines in every nook and cranny." Libby picked up a black porcelain cat and blew off the dust.

"I have to clear it all out before I can see what I need to do. I have a reseller coming in today to give me a price on taking it all away."

Libby scanned the room, taking notice of the armoires, shelves and tabletops covered with pretty little, dusty things and sighed. "Everybody in town loved Eleanor. She used to come to the café every morning before opening the store. We miss her."

"She was my favorite aunt," Steve said. "She loved this little town."

Kenji walked around. He wore Italian loafers with no socks. "Steve, do you think you can pull this together before the holidays?" He brushed at the leg of his trousers.

"The holidays? That's an aggressive schedule," Libby said. "Christmas is only six weeks away, and renovations always take longer than you and your contractor expect."

"Probate and the associated paperwork took much longer than I anticipated, too," Steve said. "I was hoping to have a gallery opening of Kenji's work, and I also want to include some of my stuff." He held up his hands, as if in defeat. "But there's so much more to do than I realized. This place is a mess."

"Exactly how much renovation are you planning on doing?" Libby asked.

"New paint and flooring, open up that storage closet," he said, pointing to a small closet that jutted into the main room. "But from there, it all depends on what the inspectors find," Steve said. "They're coming in a few days. I hope this stuff is all gone by then."

"Steve," Kenji said, "a New Year's Eve launch would be so awesome! My sculptures are almost ready. A New York gallery owner I know is going to be spending the holidays on Siesta Key. I'm sure I could get him to come to the opening. That would be so fabulous for both of us."

"That's amazing," Libby said.

Steve chuckled. "He's been stalking the guy on social media for weeks."

Kenji shook his head, rolled his eyes, and said, "I'll talk to you in a couple of days after the inspectors come by." With keys in hand, he headed for the open door.

"I think he was worried that he'd get his pants dirty," Libby said, after she heard an ignition turn over.

"He is a bit of a germophobe and quite the clothes horse, but he's not a bad guy. I've known him since college, and his work is quite good," Steve said. "And I need an artist besides myself for the grand opening."

"Do you have a contractor?"

"I was hoping to do a lot of clean-up work myself, but if the inspector finds anything serious, I'm going to have to hire an electrician and maybe a plumber," he said and sighed. "Do you happen to know any?"

"Yes, I'll give you the names of the contractors we used when we had to do repairs after the café was vandalized last summer."

"Vandalized? I thought Mariposa Beach was a sleepy little, old, Southwest Florida town."

"It is. Don't worry. Those guys are long gone."

Chapter 2

Spread the News

When Libby returned to the café, she found her neighbor, Ida Sullivan, and her white Maltese dog, Zsa Zsa, in their favorite spot in the courtyard near the fountain with the green-tailed mermaids dancing around the bowl. They were sitting just outside the café's open, sliding doors with an excellent view of the foot traffic along Mariposa Boulevard and the flags flapping on the twin, red-domed spires of the Mariposa Inn across the street. Ida was an active seventy-five, but for stability, she used a walker for support during her daily walks. The small pink pillow in the basket was for Zsa Zsa's comfort and to cushion an occasional thermos of Ida's favorite beverage.

When she saw Libby, Zsa Zsa sat up from her spot on the ground, tail wagging. Libby bent down and scratched the dog behind the ears.

"Hello, Ida. It's so good to see you and Zsa Zsa out and about on this beautiful day."

"My favorite time of year," Ida said.

Mimi appeared carrying a tray with a bowl of chili and a slice of homemade bread. She placed the food on the table in front of Ida, who closed her eyes and inhaled.

"Smells wonderful," she said.

"Libby, I was getting ready to send out the search party for you. It's almost time for me to pick up the kids from school." Mimi had two young children in elementary school.

"Did you notice the activity in Eleanor's shop?" Libby asked.

"Cheryl was in here yesterday and told me that her realty office had taken care of the closing and paperwork for Eleanor's estate," Mimi said. "She said the new owner is one of Eleanor's relatives, maybe a nephew or a cousin." She screwed up her cute little, turned-up nose, then added, "She also said that he's quite handsome." Mimi raised her eyebrows and winked.

Libby rolled her eyes as Mimi's crystal blue ones had the nerve to twinkle. Mimi was such a romantic, a walking-talking Hallmark movie in the flesh. "His name is Steve Devereaux, and he's going to open an art gallery and call it The Devereaux Gallery."

"Devereaux? That's Eleanor's maiden name," Ida said, tearing off a piece of bread and dipping it in the chili.

"He's her nephew," Libby said.

"He must be her brother's kid. Eleanor never had children of her own, and she doted on that boy. Her brother is a jerk. He lives up in Charleston. Most all the family is up there."

Ida and Eleanor had been friends for more than forty years, so she should know, Libby figured.

"I was wondering where his accent came from."

"So he's opening an art gallery?" Mimi asked.

Ida scoffed. "We already have one art gallery right here." She gestured towards the opposite corner of the courtyard.

Libby laughed and said, "Ida, The Devereaux Gallery will be at least one step above Willy's beachy art shop."

"What's he doing with all her junk?" Ida asked, between bites of chili.

"Junk? Eleanor had some cute stuff, but it's going to be hauled away by a reseller."

"I should go over to see if she has any Christmas decorations left from last year. He might sell them to me instead. Last year, I bought a cute crystal ornament with mistletoe on the top. Maybe Eleanor had things left over from last year," Mimi said, pacing back and forth between Libby and Ida, tapping her right index finger against her lips. "I'm going to put up our Christmas decorations right after Thanksgiving."

Mimi loved to decorate almost as much as she loved to bake for any holiday. Her turkey-shaped cookies flew out of the shop barely before they had a chance to cool off.

"When did you say they were coming to haul it away?"

"Soon. Steve is meeting with the resellers today."

"Eleanor will turn over in her grave when the junk man comes to haul away her stuff. I worked in her shop for years. She was always picky about where her stuff was, especially when a customer moved something from one place to another." Ida laughed. "And I don't think anyone has seen those walls in forty years."

Leaving Ida to her lunch, Libby followed Mimi back inside. Mimi set the tray on the edge of the bar. In a previous life, the café had been a tavern, and parts of the old bar were found in the café's attic. During the recent renovation, as a tribute to the building's past and because the wood was beautiful, they decided to use a portion of the bar as high-top seating against one wall and for the internet café on the opposite wall.

"Well?" Mimi asked.

"Well, what?"

"Are you suddenly blind?" Mimi asked, hands on hips. "You are no fun since you started dating the detective."

"Mimi, I wasn't crazy about you fixing me up on blind dates when I was single," Libby said, following her through the saloon doors that divided the kitchen from the cafe. "There were a few doozies, if you remember correctly."

"So, you're saying that you're not single?"

"I'm not looking for anyone else."

"You weren't looking for someone when you met Jack," Mimi continued. "Who, I might add, is a great guy, so don't screw it up." Mimi shook her finger at Libby as if she were a naughty child.

"Who me?" she asked, pointing to herself. "I can't disagree. Jack is a great guy, and, in all honestly, Steve is quite handsome, and that southern accent makes him even cuter."

"Steve?" Mimi asked. "First name basis already?"

Chapter 3

The Discovery

A few days later, Libby was on her afternoon walk to the bank and beyond, when she heard hammering and banging coming from the open door of Eleanor's Gifts, though the sign was down and the boards were pulled off the windows and leaning against the front of the building.

"Hello," Libby called out from the door.

The room, which had previously been packed from wall to wall with tables, bureaus and miscellaneous inventory was now bare except for a makeshift work table set up on saw horses. A metal tool box was open with hammers, screw drivers and various tools scattered about on the table. There were a couple of wooden dining chairs at the table. Libby remembered seeing them in Eleanor's apartment and wondered if the frilly cushions that used to occupy the chairs had gone the way of the junk man.

Steve turned and smiled. "Hello there."

"It looks bigger without all the stuff in here," Libby said, surveying the empty, dusty store.

Steve shrugged. "The last truck load got hauled away yesterday. I'm glad Mimi was able to find a few things she liked."

"A few things? She came back with two bags of stuff. It was very nice of you to give those things to her, but I have no idea what she's going to do with a whole box of mistletoe balls."

"I'm sure Aunt Eleanor would rather Mimi have them instead of an anonymous reseller, and I think the box said they were crystal ornaments adorned with mistletoe."

Libby began to laugh, pointing at the wall. "I love the way she painted around the furniture." There was a fuzzy line of soft gray that morphed to a dark blue forming the distinct outline of the furniture Eleanor had painted around.

"My Aunt Eleanor, the time saver. No one looks behind the furniture, so why move it, just paint around the cabinet. Her philosophy, not mine."

"Looks like demo day," Libby said, gesturing to the half-disassembled storage closet.

"I decided to start breaking down that closet. Once I get it cleared out, I want to go ahead and open up this room."

"I have a few minutes before I need to get back to the café," Libby said. "I can give you a hand for little while. It looks like you could use one." She reached for the hammer.

"That looks like a fresh scar on your hand. Are you sure you're up to pulling down boards and drywall?" he asked, taking her hand and looking at it.

She pulled her hand away, slipping it behind her back. "I cut myself with a knife back in August. It's healing fine. Besides, it would probably be good rehab for me to do something like this. Mimi hasn't let me handle anything sharp since the accident." Libby left out the part where she was held hostage and that she'd cut herself in the process of stabbing her captor.

"If you're sure, I could use the help."

Steve tossed her a pair of work gloves, and Libby gripped the board he had been trying to remove. He hit the other side with a hammer, and the nails finally came loose. She pulled the drywall and board off and laid it on the floor. They removed more drywall, revealing an open space between the drywall framing and a brick wall that was the main wall between Steve's building and the clothing boutique next door.

"What's this?" she asked.

"What?" Steve asked, stepping in behind her.

"There's a good deal of space in here," she said, stepping inside the area between the brick wall and where the drywall had been. "This is a false wall. Maybe it had to do with the way the closet was built."

"Wow, look at that brick. That would be an awesome accent wall," Steve said, running his fingers across the red brick. "Let's pull off some more and see what we have."

Continuing to pound and pull off drywall from the false wall, they soon uncovered insulation bunched together inside a four-by-four-foot framed-in section. They removed the boards from around the framed-in area and pulled out the insulation. When they finished pulling off all the drywall around the area, they stopped, stood back and surveyed what remained. There was rolled up plastic inside the smaller framed-in area. It was as if someone had built a compartment just for this roll of plastic tarp taped up with silver duct tape.

"What are you two doing to Eleanor's store?"

"Fletcher Smith," Libby gasped, her hand coming to her throat. "You scared the living daylights out of me."

Fletcher was in his early seventies and wore a golf shirt and a cap from the Mariposa Beach Country Club pro shop. He had just come from the café where he had had lunch with his three companions whom Libby called the 'The Company' as she was almost sure they were retired spies.

Smith introduced himself to Steve and offered his hand.

"Steve Devereaux," Steve said, pulling off his glove and shaking Smith's hand.

"What have you uncovered?" he asked, moving past them to take a closer look.

"I'm not sure. I was helping Steve remove these boards when we uncovered this plastic tarp. I'm almost afraid to go any further," Libby said.

"It's probably just a bunch of junk stuck in there," Steve said, starting to pull at the duct tape that was wound tightly around the plastic tarp. "Just like every other bit of space in this building."

"Wait," Smith said.

"Are you thinking what I'm thinking?" Libby asked. Before moving to Florida from Ohio more than three years ago, she had spent five years working in the County Prosecutor's Office.

"I think so," Smith said. "Let's proceed very carefully."

"I don't understand," Steve said, giving the tarp another yank.

"Stop," Libby called out. "Smith and I think it could be a body."

"A dead body?" Steve asked, turning from Smith to Libby. "What would a body be doing inside my wall?"

"Good question," Smith said as he picked up a box cutter from the work table and started slowly slicing through the first layer of the tarp.

"Just open it up enough for us to see what's in there," Libby said. "If it's nothing, we'll have a good laugh."

"It's probably some junk my aunt stuffed in there maybe when they built that storage closet."

"We don't know what could be in there or how long it's been in there. It could have any kind of bacteria growing in there," Smith said.

"Seriously? Why would you two think it's a body?" Steve asked.

"Past experience," Libby said. "Recent past."

"Oh, my," Steve said. "Would that have anything to do with your injured hand?"

"Inadvertently," Libby murmured, watching Smith as he carefully continued to slice the tarp, taking care not to cut too deeply while making meticulous slices with the box cutter. Finally, he cut through the edge of the tarp and the duct tape. He carefully pulled apart the edges.

When Smith uncovered an empty eye socket, Libby gasped, and Steve turned away.

A dusty, earthy, rotting smell emanated from the opening. Steve covered his mouth and choked. Libby stepped backward as her hands flew to her face covering her nose and mouth. Smith cut the tarp a little higher to reveal a skull with strands of long, blonde hair attached to a scalp that was barely clinging to the bone.

"Libby, what has taken you so long? I should have..." When she realized what she was seeing in the wall of Eleanor's gift shop, Mimi let out a blood curdling scream.

• • •

By the time Detective Jack Seiler arrived, the group inside the shop had grown. At Mimi's ear piercing scream, the sales guy from the souvenir and surf shop next door came running. He continued to hang out by the door, near enough to see what was going on yet close enough to keep an eye on the customers and the other clerk working in his store.

After Mimi stopped hyperventilating, Libby called the police. Mimi returned to the café and soon after she left, Simon Jones, the British member of Smith's little group, arrived. He was giving his assessment of the scene when Mr. Chevkov and Mr. Strauss appeared and chimed in.

"Who are these guys," Steve asked as they watched the four men examining the discovery.

"The Company," Libby said, under her breath.

"Why do you call them that?"

"Mariposa Beach, the little town where old spies come to retire," Libby said, barely loud enough for Steve to hear her.

"Oh my," Steve said. He ran his fingers across his forehead and leaned against the wall.

When Libby saw Jack Seiler in the doorway, the corners of her mouth involuntarily curved upwards. She crossed the room to meet him. "I was hoping you would catch this call."

"It's good to see you, too," he said, lightly touching her forearm, perhaps lingering a bit too long. He leaned down and whispered, "What is it with you and dead bodies and crime scenes?"

"There's no blood this time," she said, referring to the crime scene where they'd first met.

Steve offered his hand. "Hello, I'm Steve Devereaux."

"Detective Jack Seiler, Sarasota Sheriff's Department." Jack shook Steve's hand. "Who are you?"

"I own this place. We were pulling down this wall, and we found that." He gestured towards the wall.

"Looks like an old murder to me," Mr. Smith proclaimed.

"What was your first clue?" Mr. Jones asked in his crisp British accent. "The bullet hole to the head?"

"Right between the eyes," Mr. Strauss said, his faint German accent still noticeable. He held the flashlight so that Chevkov could peer inside the makeshift body bag.

"Detective, to preserve the scene, we only opened the tarp enough to see what was inside," Smith said. "We didn't want to bother you if it was nothing."

"I appreciate that, Mr. Smith."

Jack stepped up to the tarp-wrapped corpse, motioned for the people in the room to step back, then extracted rubber gloves from his pants pocket and pulled them on. He carefully slid aside the flap that Mr. Smith had cut away, but then folded back over the remains.

"Gentleman, I think you're right. I'll get the crime scene guys down here to check this out. It does look old, but in this heat, you never know. Decomposition can happen quickly."

"As soon as you start to move that skeleton, it will dearticulate," Mr. Chevkov said. "It's slightly upright only because it has been packed in there so tightly. As soon as you pull more of this packing away, the bones will fall apart."

"No one is going to touch anything until the crime scene techs get here," Jack said.

"I can't believe it."

They all turned to see Ida Sullivan standing in the doorway, pushing her walker in front of her.

"Poor thing's been here all these years."

"Ida, do you think you know who this is?" Libby asked.

"I don't think," she said. "I know." She pushed herself closer and then turned her walker around and sank onto the seat. "When I came into the café, Mimi was carrying on something fierce about what you all found in Eleanor's wall. I couldn't believe it. I had to come to see for myself."

"Mrs. Sullivan, who is it?" Jack asked, putting his hand on her shoulder.

"Annaliese Hobson and…oh my goodness, she's been in there for forty years."

Steve sank into a chair. "You mean, she was in there when Aunt Eleanor bought this place?"

"Holy Mother of God," Libby said.

Chapter 4

Photographs and Memories

Jack declared Steve's shop a crime scene, called for the Medical Examiner and Crime Scene Techs and began to take witness statements. Steve drove Libby and Ida back to Ida's house to find a photo of Annaliese.

Libby was worried about Ida's heart. She had had some health problems recently, and Libby thought that getting her away from the crime scene and concentrating on the task of searching through her boxes of photos would help calm her.

They were sitting at Ida's dining room table with six shoe boxes of photographs going back sixty years. Ida opened the first box and spread the photos across the table. ZsaZsa ran around their feet, sniffing and barking at Steve, a new person invading her domain.

"Annaliese's mother's name was Mary Alice. She, Eleanor and I were good friends. Mary Alice died of breast cancer when Annaliese was about twelve and going into the years when a girl needs her mother."

Libby picked up a black and white 8x10 photograph of a showgirl dressed in a glittery costume and wearing a huge feather headdress in the shape of a fan. "Is this you?" she asked, holding the photo up for Ida to see.

Ida nodded and went back to emptying the shoe box.

Steve took the photo, looked at Ida, and back to the picture, and then asked, "Mrs. Sullivan, you were a Rockette?"

Libby met his gaze and raised her eyebrows.

Ida nodded. "A lifetime ago, but I could do a pretty good high kick in my day."

She took the photo, set it aside and continued her story, "The Hobson family owned most of this town and were bigwigs way back before there was even a Sarasota County. They owned the Mariposa Inn when it was nothing more than a pit stop on the trail." She shuffled through the pictures and held up a photo of the Inn with an old sedan sitting at the curb. "They owned the whole block where Eleanor's shop was. It used to be a general store. You know, like a five and dime."

She shuffled through another stack of pictures before she continued, "After Mary Alice died, Albert pretty much ignored the girl. He just went about running his businesses and catting around town. Eleanor and I tried to be there for her, but…" Her voice trailed off.

"What do you think happened to Annaliese?" Libby asked.

Ida continued her story as if she hadn't heard Libby, at all. "Annaliese was a beautiful girl with that white blonde hair and bright blue eyes." She looked up at Libby. "Mimi reminds me a little bit of her, just in looks. Mimi can be a bit flighty. Annaliese was more free-spirited."

Libby smiled at the description.

Ida sighed, opened another shoebox and began to shuffle through the contents. "I keep saying that I'm going to put these in a photo album, but…Here it is. I knew I had a picture of her." She held up a black and white photo of a young girl of about seventeen with long, pale blonde hair. She wore cutoff jeans and a flowy peasant blouse. She stood in front of a large, two-story brick house with pillars and a veranda.

"That's the big house a few miles up the beach," Libby said.

"That's the old Hobson house. The estate used to be much bigger and included horse barns and beautiful lawns. It was a showcase. But after she disappeared, Albert was rattling around that house all by himself. When he died, what was left of the place sold at auction. I always hoped that Annaliese was out there somewhere, living her life far away from her ass of a father. Albert Hobson sure was a mean old bastard."

"What do you think happened?" Steve asked.

"Albert said she ran off with a circus boy, but if that's her in your wall, Albert must have killed her in a fit of rage. He had a terrible temper."

"A circus boy?" Libby asked. "Do you remember his name?"

"I only met the boy once. My husband, his name was Sid, was an accountant. He worked for Hobson's. We went to the big house for parties and such. When Mary Alice was alive, they had glorious parties." Ida's eyes welled with her memories.

"That must have been beautiful," Libby said, patting her hand.

Ida nodded and continued her story, "After Mary Alice died, Albert still had Christmas parties for his employees but not like when Mary Alice was alive. The time I met the boy was at the employee Christmas party in early December, just a week or so before she disappeared."

"What happened?" Steve asked.

"Annaliese loved the horses, and this boy worked for the horse trainer at the circus." She looked at Steve and then said, "You know Sarasota is a big circus town, right?"

Steve smiled. "I heard that somewhere."

"Albert wanted her to make an appearance at the party. It was a tradition for the whole Hobson family to be at the Christmas party. But, she was in the barn with her sick horse and that boy and the vet. Albert went into a rage. It was a terrible row. She was devastated. I felt bad for her. A week later, she was gone."

"And everyone thought she ran away with the boy," Libby said.

"That's about it," Ida said.

"It's too bad we don't know his name," Libby said.

"Maybe if I saw him, it might jog my memory, so I'll look through these pictures some more." She handed the photo of Annaliese to Libby. "Here, give this to your detective."

"Thanks, I will. I'm sure Jack will get it back to you as soon as he can."

Ida met Libby's eyes with a look of recognition. "I just realized something. That was the last Hobson family Christmas party."

• • •

Libby and Steve left Ida searching through her photos for pictures of the party.

"*Your* detective?" Steve asked.

"Yeah, well, that's another story, but I should probably drop into the café. It's been a long time since I left for the bank."

"Okay." He started the car. "Do you think Mimi is all right? I don't think I've ever heard such a scream. My ears are still ringing."

"Mimi has a big voice. Her parents are into opera." Libby motioned for Steve to pull into the parking lot behind the cafe. "Let's go in the back through the kitchen."

The kitchen was a square room with a rectangular prep table in the middle and an industrial-sized refrigerator against the opposite wall. The wall to the right of the back door held a grill, stove, sink and work counter.

Libby heard voices in the café and pushed the saloon doors open to find the cafe quite busy. Mimi and Louisa were working behind the counter. Lisa, the part time afternoon barista, was at the cappuccino machine.

"Libby, I heard you found another dead body," Lisa said.

She was a tiny young woman with a curly brown bob who was always full of questions and witty comments.

"Another body?" Steve asked.

Before Libby could answer, Mimi asked, "How is Ida?"

"She's looking through old photos hoping to find any that could help identify the remains," Libby said. "Did you know that Ida was a Rockette?"

"No! Are you serious?" Mimi asked, blue eyes widened.

"She sure was a looker," Steve said. "I'm hungry. Can I order something?" He stepped around the counter and picked up a menu.

"Rachel," Lisa called out. "Here's your cappuccino."

Rachel, a young woman with a long dark ponytail and big brown eyes, stepped up to the counter next to Steve. "Excuse me," she said.

"Oh, sorry," Steve said. He looked up from his menu and added, "Hello."

"Rachel, this is Steve. He bought Eleanor's shop," Libby said.

"I think you should ask Rachel to smudge your store or do something to chase away any bad mojo," Mimi said.

Rachel read Tarot Cards on Saturday evenings at the café and was in the process of opening a new shop across the courtyard from the cafe.

"Pardon me?" Steve asked.

"It's done to clear the space of any negative energy," Rachel explained. "Mimi told me about your wall. I'm going to cleanse my place of anything left over from the accessories shop."

The previous owner had a run of bad luck, bankruptcy, and had to close the shop in the space that now housed The Mariposa Mystic, Rachel's new shop.

"That might be a good idea, considering what we just found," Libby said. "That is, if you believe in that sort of thing."

Turning to Steve, coffee cup in hand, Rachel said, "Once the police and crime scene people are finished, I'd be happy to smudge your shop. I have everything I need, but I need to finish unpacking to find it."

"I'm so excited that we'll have two new shops this season," Mimi said. "That's more hungry customers for the café."

"When are you opening?" Steve asked.

"The grand opening is planned for Black Friday."

Mimi held up her coffee cup. "Here's to The Devereaux Gallery and The Mariposa Mystic. Welcome to the neighborhood."

Chapter 5

Return to the Scene of the Crime

When Libby and Steve returned to the gallery, the crime scene techs were carefully moving the tarp-wrapped remains to a body bag for transport to the county morgue. Jack Seiler was speaking with one of the techs, a tall woman with a camera in her hands, the strap around her neck. She gestured toward the area where the tarp had been securely built into the wall and then showed him a picture on her camera. Once the techs removed the body, she returned to the location and took more photos of what was, in effect, a tomb.

Jack joined Steve and Libby near the gallery door, where they were watching the activity.

"Any luck with Ida's photos?" Jack asked.

"This is the girl she thinks was in that wall." Libby handed Jack the photograph of Annaliese standing in front of the Hobson house.

"Pretty girl," Jack said. "Anything else?"

"Ida was a Rockette," Libby said.

"Seriously?"

Libby nodded. "Skimpy costume, feather headdress. The works."

"Wow!" He thought for a minute. "Knowing Ida Sullivan, I'm not surprised."

Steve stood, hands on hips, off to the side, watching the two crime scene technicians zip up the black body bag. He walked to the back of the room and stood at the door to the parking lot where the ME's van was parked, back doors open. He held the door as the two crime scene techs wheeled out the gurney and loaded it into the van. The photographer was still snapping photos, inside the framed-in space as well as along the wall that Steve and Libby had pulled down.

"When can I start working on my gallery again?" Steve asked.

"It shouldn't be long," Jack said. "It looks like the crime was more than forty years ago, but we still have to wait for the ME to examine the remains."

"Cause of death should be easy," Libby said. "Bullet hole to the head."

"They'll have to try to identify her," Jack said.

"Will that picture we got from Mrs. Sullivan help at all?" Steve asked.

"Yes, it should. Hopefully, we can get some DNA from the bones, too," Jack said.

"And if there's some living relative, perhaps that would help identify if she is Annaliese Hobson," Libby added.

"I'm never going to make that gallery opening," Steve said, hanging his head.

"If they lift the crime scene soon, I'm sure we can get this place ready for New Year's Eve," Libby said. "I'll be glad to help you out. I've been helping Rachel get her shop ready, and now I can help you."

"New Year's Eve?" Jack asked. "That's only about five weeks away."

"I know, and now with the gallery being a crime scene, I don't know how we can make it."

"Don't give up," Libby said.

"Hey, Seiler. I'm done here." The crime scene photographer walked towards them, her pack slung onto her back. The woman was almost as tall as Jack. Her dark hair was pulled into a tight bun.

"Thanks, Ellen." He introduced Libby and Steve to Ellen Sanders.

"Did I hear you say that you're going to open a gallery in here?" Ellen asked.

"Yes, I was hoping to do a launch on New Year's Eve, but now, I'm not so sure." Steve shook his head and surveyed the room. "There's a lot to do and now...all this."

"Let me know when you have your launch," Ellen said. "I'll be there."

• • •

After leaving Steve with instructions not to touch, move or remove anything on the first floor, Libby and Jack started walking towards the café.

"Are you hungry?" Libby asked. "I can fix you something at the café or my house."

"Not right now, maybe later. First, I'd like to stop by Ida's house."

As they crossed Mariposa Boulevard and headed up North Shell Street towards Ida's house, Libby asked, "What was that with the photographer?"

"What do you mean?"

"When Steve and I arrived, you and she were in a discussion, and she was pointing towards the remains. Then, she showed you a picture on her camera."

"We were discussing the placement and condition of the remains."

"The way the body was stuffed into that framed-in section of the false wall seemed planned out, not spontaneous or in the moment," Libby said.

"It's likely that she was killed someplace else and brought here after she was mostly decomposed."

"Now that I think about it, in this heat and humidity, she would have been a soupy, smelly mess if she were entombed in that wall…uh…fresh," Libby said, shuddering at the thought.

"Ida is the only person I know who lived here forty years ago," Jack said as they turned toward Ida's house. "Perhaps she can remember what was going on with that building before Eleanor bought it."

• • •

Ida lived across the street from Libby in the Mariposa Beach neighborhood originally platted in 1899, at least that's what was on the historical marker at the corner of North Shell and Palmetto Street. Many of the homes were remodeled tourist cottages. Ida's was one of the larger houses on the block. It was painted pale pink with white shutters and trim. Pink was Ida's favorite color.

Zsa Zsa greeted their knock with a happy bark. She was excited to see Jack and leapt at the sight of him. The dog was crazy about him, her little stump of a tail wagging with joy.

Ida was still hard at work, sorting through pictures. She tossed anything she thought relevant to the town, the buildings or the Hobson family in a separate box and stacked other photos on the table in neat little piles.

"Ida, you sure have a lot of pictures," Jack remarked, scratching Zsa Zsa's ears.

"I like pictures," she said with a little smile. "There's seventy-five years' worth of memories in these boxes."

"Is this Eleanor's building?" Libby asked. The picture in her hand was of the block that currently included The Village Dress Shoppe, Eleanor's Gifts, now The Devereaux Gallery, and the Surf Shop.

"It was Hobson's Five and Dime back then. They bought both buildings and knocked out the wall to include Eleanor's shop and that beach store. They closed the wall back up when Hobson closed the Five and Dime and opened the supermarket back in the late seventies."

"So, the building was empty before Eleanor bought it?" Jack asked.

"Yes, it was empty for quite a while. Albert and his brother, Harry, owned that whole block. Harry had a real estate office at the far end where that overpriced dress shop is now. There's no apartment above that end building, just a storage attic."

"Do you remember when Annaliese disappeared?" Jack asked.

"I surely do," Ida said. "It was right around Christmas 1978."

"After that party, you were telling Steve and me about?" Libby asked.

Ida nodded and pushed a stack of photos towards Libby. "Here are some pictures we took at that party. Sid had just bought me a camera for Christmas, and we were trying it out that day."

They sorted through color photos of the holiday lawn party. Picnic tables were set up under a striped tent with a bar across from it on the side lawn of the house. Tables and chairs were scattered about the yard, and servers carried trays of drinks and food. In one picture facing the road, Libby thought she saw a sliver of beach in the background.

Ida held up a photo of a woman in a robin's egg-blue chiffon dress, gathered at the waist and bust with short cap sleeves. "Sid was trying out the camera and was asking me to pose and then he'd change the settings, make a note, and then take another picture." Ida pushed forward six more photos of herself in various locations.

"Gorgeous dress," Libby said.

"Mrs. Sullivan, you were a knock out," Jack said. "Sid was a lucky man to have you on his arm."

She laughed and held up another photo. "This is Albert Hobson."

In the picture, Ida's outstretched hand held a drink as did the man with his arm around her waist. He wore dark trousers, a white button-down shirt with the sleeves rolled up and his necktie loosened. Libby estimated he was in his late fifties.

"He's standing a little close there," Jack said, taking the photo from her hand. "What did Sid think about that?"

"There were rumors about Hobson even before Mary Alice died. You know, womanizing." Ida raised her eyebrows and looked from Jack to Libby. "There were even more rumors after she died. Sid knew he didn't have to worry about me, besides, I was probably too old for Albert's tastes. He liked them younger, if you catch my drift."

Jack handed the photo to Libby and said, "Ida, you said that Mr. Hobson and Annaliese argued that day."

"Yes, soon after Sid took this picture." Ida retrieved the picture of her and Hobson from Libby and picked up a magnifying glass from the table. "Look in the background. I think that is Annaliese and the boy I was telling you about."

Libby took the glass and the photo. Jack stood, and with his hand on her shoulder, he leaned over her to see the picture. "The girl in the white dress or this one? There appears to be someone else in the corner of the photo, but it's cut off."

"Yes, the girl in the dress," Ida said. She pointed at the picture. "They are heading towards the barn. She's in her party dress because her father ordered her to make an appearance, but her horse was sick, and she would have rather been in the barn. Right after this picture, Albert caught a glance of her heading towards the barn in that dress, and he took out after her."

"What happened?" Libby asked.

"I followed him, and Sid followed me. We could hear Albert hollering and yelling at her before we even got to the barn. When I reached the door, he had a horsewhip in his hands, and the vet had a hold of him so that he wouldn't hit the boy or Annaliese."

"No wonder she wanted to run away," Libby said.

"She was crying, and the boy was trying to protect her by pushing her behind him. It was an awful scene. The vet told the boy to leave, and he did. Annaliese ran into the house. Albert's sister, Harriet, and I went to check on her awhile later. She was in her room crying, so we just let her be."

"What was it about the boy that had her father ready to horsewhip him?" Jack asked, standing up and walking around the small dining area.

"Albert didn't think the boy was good enough for his daughter. The boy worked with the horse trainer at the circus and the vet."

"Are you sure that Annaliese and the boy were romantically involved?" Jack asked.

"Well, other than that day, I only saw them together maybe one other time that I remember. It was just a few days after that party, and I was walking Zsa Zsa The First down along the beach road."

At the mention of her name, Zsa Zsa lifted her head. Seeing nothing, she laid back down in her place at Jack's feet.

Ida continued, "I saw them ahead of me walking towards the beach. They were holding hands, so I figured they were going steady or something. I walked on over to the beach, and I turned up Mariposa Boulevard. I guess that was the last time I saw her, that is…until today."

"Did you ever see the boy again?" Jack asked.

"Nope, never did. I guess that's why it was so easy to believe that they ran off together." Ida leaned back in her chair and shook her head. "This breaks my heart."

"Ida, I'm so sorry," Libby said, placing her hands over Ida's.

"Don't jump to conclusions now. It may not even be her," Jack said, returning to his seat at the table. "I think we are going to need DNA to verify her identity."

"I would imagine there are some cousins around here. His brother had four kids, and I'm sure they've married and had kids," Ida said.

She shuffled through the photos and came up with a picture of a man who looked a bit younger than Hobson with a woman and four children who appeared to range from about six to sixteen. "This is his brother, Harry, and his family. I can't remember his wife's name, maybe Joan or Jeanne. She could be a real snake in the grass."

Ida made a 'tsk, tsk, tsk' sound, and Libby stifled a giggle.

"I think I heard that Harry died a few years back."

"You mentioned a sister. Do you know where she is?" Jack asked.

"The last I heard she was still over on the east coast, maybe Boca or Lauderdale," Ida said. "I'll look around. I might have an old Christmas card with an address on it."

"That would be great." Jack thumbed through his notebook, then returned it to his jacket pocket. He felt the picture that Libby had given him earlier. He pulled the picture of Annaliese out of his pocket. "Thanks for this picture." He started to return it to his pocket, but stopped and examined it closer. "You know, I've been to this house."

"When was that?" Libby asked.

"I was about fourteen or fifteen. I went there with my dad for an auction of some of their equipment. Growing up on a ranch, we were always looking for a good deal at auctions and sales. If I remember correctly, they were selling off a parcel of land that included some of the outbuildings."

"His whole estate was sold off, piece by piece," Ida said.

Jack returned the photograph and his notebook to his jacket pocket. "I think we've bothered you enough this afternoon. If I have any more questions, I'll call or come by again. All right?"

"Come by anytime. Zsa Zsa likes you." Zsa Zsa barked in agreement.

Libby picked up a photo of Ida in the blue dress standing in front of a palm tree with Christmas lights wrapped around it and a man dressed in a Santa Claus suit. "I just love that dress."

"I did, too," Ida said. "I was about thirty-five or thirty-six that year."

"I just realized the age you were then is the same age we are now," Jack said.

"Speak for yourself," Libby said. "I won't be thirty-five for six months."

• • •

Once outside, Jack took her hand. "I'll walk you home."

"All the way across the street." Libby loved the way he slipped his hand around hers, like a mitten on a chilly day.

He was silent as they walked the short distance to her home, built in the 1940s by a boat captain and renovated into a cozy beach cottage by the previous owners. She unlocked the back door, and they were barely inside the kitchen before he pulled her to him, backed her up against the door and kissed her hard.

Breathless, he said, "I have wanted to kiss you all afternoon. I find it hard to keep my hands off you, even while I'm working."

"It's hard to be professional when the thoughts running through my mind involve throwing myself into your arms," she said. "Probably doesn't do much for your tough guy detective look, either."

He kissed her again, his hands in her hair. She slipped her hands under his shirt and as she skipped her fingers up his back, she felt his body slightly shudder.

"As much as I would love to stay," he said, kissing her again, "I need to get back to the department to file this report and see what's going on there."

"You are such a tease. You come over to my house, kiss me all over and then leave." She giggled as he kissed her neck. "This is one of the reasons I had that rule about dating cops, which I have so soundly broken with you."

"And I am so grateful you did. I'll call you later." He gave her a devilish grin. "And I will make it up to you, I promise."

"I'll walk with you, ok? I should stop in the cafe. I've been shirking my duties this afternoon working your case."

"You loved it, and you know it," he said.

He was right, she thought. She did enjoy working a case. She missed that part of her old life more than she could admit, even to herself.

He tucked in his shirt and finger-combed his black hair. Then kissed her one more time before opening the door.

Libby followed him outside, locked the door, then turned to him and said, "I hope we can get DNA evidence to find out if that is Annaliese Hobson."

"We'll be fortunate to get anything usable from that skeleton. Maybe from the bone marrow. They've actually gotten DNA from skeletons that are much older than forty years," Jack said. "So, maybe we'll get lucky."

"What about from the hair?" Libby asked. "There were strands of long blonde hair on what was left of the scalp."

"Perhaps, if there are follicles left. But don't get your hopes up."

He slipped his hand into hers as they walked across the street and turned towards the café.

"Do you want a cup of coffee for the road?" she asked. "Or a sandwich? You haven't eaten anything. You must be starving."

"How about a sandwich to go," he said. "And throw in some cookies. I'll share them with Sam, if he's still in the office."

Sam Stacey was Jack's partner.

"Where is Sam?" she asked.

"He's running down some leads on another case. He said he thought I could handle a skeleton in a wall all by myself."

Chapter 6

Time Line

Later that evening, Libby sat at her desk, laptop open, a blank legal pad beside her and a cold Corona in her hand. She had a copy of Ida's photograph of Annaliese. That afternoon, while Steve was eating his sandwich, she had taken the picture into her office and made a photocopy.

She set the beer on the table and picked up the red stress ball prescribed as rehab for her injured hand. She examined the scar in her palm. With her left forefinger, she traced the bumpy scar where the surgeon had repaired the tendons and stitched up the knife wound. She transferred the ball to her right hand and closed her healing fingers around the ball, knowing that, though she still experienced some stiffness, she was fortunate to have regained a good deal of functionality. She began to squeeze the ball as she'd found that the absentminded squeezing motion also helped her think.

She was puzzled by the time line. How could a dead body be in a wall for forty years without being detected? In the beginning, there must have been some odor, even if the body was mostly decomposed before being placed inside the wall. Although the real estate office, now the dress shop, was a separate but conjoined building, they must have smelled something.

They probably thought a raccoon crawled into the empty building, got trapped, and died.

With the thick brick wall separating the two shops, the sealed up tarp and the insulation they found surrounding the body, Libby wondered if perhaps that was enough to keep the lingering smell of a decomposing body to a minimum.

Her attention turned to the overpriced dress shop, as Ida called it. How long had that shop been open? Harry Hobson's real estate office had been there at least into the late seventies or the early eighties. There must have been other businesses in that building in between.

Perhaps I can do a computer search to find out what was in that space between the real estate office and the dress shop.

Maybe that's why Eleanor started burning candles, to cover up the lingering smell.

Before moving to Florida a little more than three years ago, Libby was an attorney working in the Clermont County Prosecutor's Office near Cincinnati, Ohio. A big believer in visuals and the need to get her head around the time lines of a case, it had always helped her to draw it out. Deciding a time line was in order, she drew a line on her legal pad. She wrote 'Nov. 2019' above the line on the right side. Below the line, she wrote 'body discovered.'

If Annaliese was seventeen when she disappeared in December 1978, then she was born in 1961. She wrote '1961' at the left hand side. Libby decided to put in as many dates as she could now, and then fill in the specific dates as she was able to verify them. She added 'Dec 1978' about two inches to the right and wrote 'Annaliese disappears' below it.

Steve closed on the building in late October, so she added a tick just to the left of the 'Nov 2019', labeled it 'Oct 2019', 'Steve closes on the building.' According to Steve and Ida, Eleanor's shop had been in that location for forty years. But,

~ 36 ~

when exactly did Eleanor take possession of that building, Libby wondered. Was it a full forty years or about forty years? Libby decided that forty years could, in reality, be between thirty-nine and forty-one years, meaning that Eleanor could have taken possession anywhere been 1978 and 1980, but if Annaliese disappeared in December 1978, it was most likely not 1978.

About midway down the page on the legal pad, she wrote 'Questions.' Under it, she wrote 'When did Eleanor close on the building?' She would ask Steve that question as he should have that information in his aunt's papers. She looked at her watch. It was nearly ten o'clock. A little late to call tonight. She would ask him about that tomorrow.

She remembered the old picture Ida had of the Inn. She went to the Mariposa Inn website and discovered they opened in September 1977 after purchasing the old Hobson Inn in 1976. After a significant renovation, they reopened as the Mariposa Inn. The old photos on the website revealed that they must have made additional improvements over the years because the hotel was now more extensive with the lobby expansion and the addition of the Veranda Bar, though the original, twin, red-domed spires and the red tile roof were well preserved. She added this information to her time line.

As she added more entries to the time line, she realized that the missing information surrounding how long the building was empty was key to determining when the body could have been placed there. Also, she had questions about renovations in the building. Who did the construction to split the original shop into two shops and who put them back together?

Libby leaned back in her chair, stretched her back and yawned. Her phone rang, and Jack's name displayed. She smiled as she answered.

"Hello."

"Hey, what are you doing?" he asked.

"I'm sitting in my living room drinking a beer. You?"

"I'm sitting on my porch drinking a beer."

"What did you find out?" she asked.

"Not much. I completed my reports, and that's about it. By the way, Sam thanks you for the cookies."

"I'm glad he enjoyed them," she said, then added, "I was just wondering how could a body have been in that wall all these years without someone noticing some kind of odor, even if it was mostly or even partially decomposed when it was entombed?"

"Good question, but if the building sat empty a significant amount of time, then when Eleanor moved in, perhaps it wasn't as noticeable," Jack said.

"Ida said that Eleanor always had candles and such burning. Perhaps that was a habit started because of a funky smell when she moved in."

"We'll never know," Jack said. "Eleanor can't tell us, and not too many people are going to remember much other than Eleanor liked to burn candles."

"I know," she said. "The time line is a puzzle."

"You do like a mystery."

"I want answers," she said.

"Don't we all," he said.

"Thanksgiving is next week," she said. "Are you going to your father's?"

Jack's mother had died more than a decade prior. Libby knew he was the youngest of five, with two older brothers and two older sisters.

"I hope so, but I'm on call. Is Julia having dinner?"

Libby's Aunt Julia lived with her son, David, on Longboat Key, about forty minutes north of Mariposa Beach. "Yes, actually, my mother is coming down from Ohio. I hope you will be able to meet her while she's here."

~ 38 ~

"I hope so, too," he said. "Please be careful poking around in old family secrets. They have a habit of coming to light in unpleasant ways."

They chatted for a few more minutes. He promised to call her the next day, and then, after sweet goodnights, they hung up.

• • •

Early the next morning, Libby walked into the café to the glorious smells of baking pastries and morning coffee. Louisa had been baking since before five o'clock. Scones, muffins and cookies were already in the display case. Libby loved mornings in the café. They opened at seven, and usually, hungry patrons waited at the door to pick up a cup of coffee, a scone or a breakfast sandwich on the way to work or school.

Mimi flew in the back door a few minutes behind Libby. "I'm so sorry. I overslept."

"You're not late," Libby said, handing her a cup of coffee. "We have ten minutes before we turn on the lights and open the doors."

"I barely slept. I kept seeing that horrible face in my dreams." She took a sip of coffee. "That tastes so good. I jumped out of bed, ran through the shower, jumped into my clothes and now I'm here. Paul is getting the kids ready for school. Thank goodness podiatrist's office hours aren't this early."

"Take a breath," Libby said and laughed.

"I am so glad that I did not see that horrible thing," Louisa said, her brown eyes squinted. "So scary."

She placed a cookie sheet of turkey-shaped sugar cookies on the prep table. After they cooled, Mimi would spend the morning icing and decorating them.

Libby pushed through the saloon doors into the café. She was proud of what she and Mimi had accomplished in the almost three years that the restaurant had been open. The Mariposa Café had been Mimi's dream. Libby had moved to Florida after being shot by a ricocheted bullet during a police operation that had involved her now ex-husband, Tony. She was recuperating at her Aunt Julia's house on Longboat Key, spending her days sitting on the beach gazing out to sea. A chance trip to Mariposa Beach for an art fair led to an introduction to Mimi. Mimi needed someone to help her with a business plan, Libby had the time and a divorce settlement. They became partners, and the Mariposa Café was born.

A knock on the door brought her back to the present. Taryn Bellingham's round face peered through the door. She was pointing at her watch. Libby laughed, flipped on the lights and opened the door to start the day.

About ten o'clock, Libby was clearing and wiping tables when Steve came in, somewhat bleary-eyed, wearing a wrinkled T-shirt and the same cargo shorts he'd worn the day before.

"Coffee," he muttered.

"Did you have trouble sleeping?" Libby asked, going behind the counter to pour the coffee.

Steve collapsed onto the leather sofa. "I couldn't stay in my apartment. There's still too much of Eleanor there, even after I threw out all of her shabby chic stuff."

Libby handed him the coffee, and he took a long gulp. "I tried to sleep, but I kept thinking about the girl in the wall, all the work I have to do in the gallery, the launch, and, on top of all of that, my mother wants me to come home for Thanksgiving."

"I'm sorry you didn't sleep well," Libby said. "You and Mimi have something in common. She didn't sleep well last night, either."

"I finally gave up," he said. "I got a room at the Inn at about ten o'clock last night. I slept like the dead. Sorry, poor choice of words. I just now woke up."

"Can I get you something to eat?" she asked. "The breakfast sandwiches are delicious. I can ask Louisa to make you one."

"That sounds awesome." He laid his head on the back of the sofa and closed his eyes.

By the time she returned with the sandwich, he had moved to a table and was reading the morning paper. She set the sandwich on the table and retrieved a pot of coffee to refresh his cup.

"This is delicious," he said. "Hits the spot."

Libby set the coffee pot on the table, but before she could sit down, Fletcher Smith called from the corner, "Libby, can you refresh mine, too?"

"Of course," she said, retrieving the coffee pot.

Smith, Jones, Strauss and Chevkov were having their regular Friday morning breakfast discussion, heads together, voices low to limit eavesdropping from neighboring tables. Today's conversation involved the possible identity of the person in the wall and how she happened to be there in the first place.

"Have you heard anything from the detective about the remains in Eleanor's shop?" Jones asked.

He had curly dark hair sprinkled with gray giving him an aristocratic air that, along with his British accent and the twinkle in his eye, reminded her of an older version of the actor, Hugh Grant.

"Not really, and I haven't heard from him this morning," Libby said, refilling their cups.

"Because of the condition of the remains," Chevkov said, "we believe she must have been killed elsewhere and moved to this location."

He was lean and balding with piercing, ice blue eyes.

"Jack mentioned that possibility last night," Libby said. "The remains are with the ME now."

"You will let us know if you find out anything, won't you?" Smith asked.

"Of course," Libby said.

She returned to Steve's table, where he had finished his sandwich and returned to reading the paper.

"Steve, do you mind if I sit down for a minute?" she asked. "I have something I want to ask you."

"Ask away," he said, putting down the paper.

"Do you have your aunt's papers that identify exactly when she bought the building?"

"Yes, I do. Why do you ask?"

"I was working out a time line last night."

"And?"

"I'm trying to establish exactly how long the building was empty. That can help us narrow down the window of opportunity for when the body could have been placed inside the wall. So, if we know when she bought the building and opened the store, as well as when Hobson closed his store, then we have that piece of the time line."

"I see. Do you know when Hobson closed his store?"

"I looked it up online last night." Libby leaned forward. "Hobson's Market opened in January 1978 out by the highway. That means the Five and Dime here in Mariposa Beach must have closed in late 1977."

"So, depending on when Aunt Eleanor opened her store, that could help determine when the body was placed in the wall," he said.

"Exactly. Jack says that she was most likely killed somewhere else and then placed in the wall sometime later, after she had mostly decomposed, otherwise, there would have been a lot more…uh…stuff in there."

"That sounds disgusting," Steve said.

"Sorry to ruin your breakfast, but decomposing bodies are disgusting."

"Sounds like you know from experience."

"It's a long story that…"

"I need an Almond Coconut Dream Latte," Rachel announced, referring to one of Mariposa Café's specialty coffee drinks, as she came in from the courtyard door.

Libby stood up and went to make her latte. "Opening day nerves?"

Rachel groaned in response and plopped into the chair that Libby had vacated.

"Hi. Steve, isn't it?"

Steve nodded. "So, you're opening next Friday?"

"I'm going to do a soft opening this Saturday. Black Friday will be the grand opening launch."

"Congratulations," Steve said. "I'll be there."

Libby arrived with the latte and set it on the table in front of Rachel.

"Did you decide not to go to your mother's for Thanksgiving?" Libby asked Steve.

"I just don't have the time, especially if I can be working in the shop."

Rachel held the coffee mug in both hands, closed her eyes and inhaled. "Ahhhh. Heaven. Chocolate, almond and coconut. The nectar of the gods."

• • •

Detective Sam Stacey, a cup of hot coffee in hand, slipped into his office chair across from his partner, Detective Jack Seiler.

"What 'cha got here?"

"It's a preliminary report on the skeleton in the wall," Jack said, holding up the document. "The ME's office just faxed it over."

"That was quick," Stacey said, taking the report from Jack. "Not much here."

"They gave the skeleton the once over first thing this morning. They were hoping to get some DNA to help with identification."

"Were they able to get any?" Sam asked, flipping through the pages.

"They think so, from the bones, and they found some follicles on a few of the hair strands. They've sent it off to the lab, but I think it's probably a long shot, at best."

"There's animal and insect evidence, so that proves your theory that the body was someplace else before it was sealed up in that wall," Sam said.

"But where?" Jack asked. "And why was it moved?"

"Perhaps something was going on with the old location that would cause the discovery of the body, so they had to find a new place to stash it."

"Like an auction?" Jack muttered.

Sam leaned forward. "What?"

"Never mind. We need to find some Hobson relatives for comparison," Jack said. "Without the comparisons, we have nothing. There's no way Annaliese Hobson's DNA, from forty years ago, would be in any database."

"That's who Ida Sullivan thinks was in that wall?" Sam asked.

"Yes, Ida was pretty shaken up about this. She knew the family. But it could just be a coincidence that the Hobson girl disappeared around the same time the building was empty."

"You're right. It could be someone else. Have you looked through the old missing persons' cold cases?" Sam asked.

"That's what I was doing before I got this report," Jack said, taking the report back and turning to the last page. "So far, no luck."

"Something's bothering you," Sam said, taking another sip of coffee. "You have that look on your face."

"Possible fetal remains. There were a few, small, extra bones that indicate the girl in the wall may have been pregnant."

"That would be a motive for murder, especially if it were someone like one of the Hobson brothers. They wouldn't want an illegitimate child running around."

"We don't know it even was the Hobsons. It could have been someone who knew the building was empty and under construction. Maybe someone on the work crew," Jack said. "A good drywall guy could have built that compartment and drywalled it up without anyone the wiser."

"This is a forty-year-old cold case. How are we going to get that kind of information? Who worked on a construction crew or who knew what when? It's hard enough with a current case, much less one this cold." Sam leaned back in his chair.

"You're right, but that's not what's got me bothered," Jack said.

"Another case?"

"No, Libby is going to ask about the ME report, and I don't want to tell her what the ME found."

"You don't have to tell her anything."

Jack laughed. "You know her. When she gets involved in something, she's like a dog with a bone. She won't let it go until she gets the information she wants."

"Like when she figured out that money laundering scheme, gave us the slip and went to Key West alone last August?" Sam asked. "She's a smart cookie." He laughed. "Hell, she could probably solve this case for you."

"Very funny."

"Why wouldn't you tell her?" Sam asked. "This isn't a high priority case. We may never figure out whose bones those are."

"Remember Libby was shot back in Ohio? In that stake out gone bad?"

"Yeah, but I'm not connecting the dots between our victim and Libby."

"Libby was pregnant when she was shot. She blames herself for losing the baby," Jack said.

"Wow. I see what you mean, partner. This news could make her even more determined to figure out what happened."

"She comes across as strong and confident, but there's a side of her that can be quite melancholy," Jack said. "I ran into that old guy, Mr. Mendelson, at the café awhile ago. He lives next door to Libby's aunt. He said Libby was pretty much a basket case when she first moved down here."

"Man, you've got it bad for her," Sam said.

"Yeah, and there's that." Jack tossed the report on his desk and leaned forward towards Sam. "Don't tell her I told you this."

"Jack, trust me, don't tell her what's in the report."

Chapter 7

Make the Call

Steve called later that afternoon and said that, according to the deed, Eleanor closed on her store November 1, 1979, and the grand opening was February 14, 1980 with a Valentine's Day theme. He found some old flyers in with his aunt's papers advertising the big event. He also found blueprints and construction plans that showed the renovations were completed on the building before Eleanor took possession.

Libby filled-in the dates on her time line. Annaliese disappeared in December 1978, her father closed the Five and Dime in late 1977, and Eleanor opened the store in 1980. That meant the building was empty about fourteen months, more than enough time to hide a body and let nature take its course, so to speak, in the decomposition part.

Libby looked through her phone until she found the number she needed. She started to tap the call button, but instead, went to the refrigerator and opened a Corona. She took a long pull. After a deep breath and only a moment's hesitation, she tapped the call icon.

"Red, how ya' doin'?"

"Ray Ban, my man. I'm doing good." Libby couldn't help but smile at the thought of Ray Ban sitting in front of his bay of computer monitors, answering the phone, sunglasses on regardless of the lighting.

"Good to hear your voice," he said.

Libby met Ray Ban at the University of Cincinnati when they were undergrads. He had a gift for locating information. As far as his methods, Libby believed in the 'don't ask; don't tell' philosophy of life. It gave her plausible deniability, at least that's what she told herself.

"Back at you, my friend."

"What can I do for you, Red?"

He was the only person who got away with calling her 'Red' and she let him do it for old time's sake.

"I need you to do some background research for me. The family name is Hobson. The man's name is Albert. Brother is Harry. Annaliese Hobson is Albert's daughter. Everybody thought she ran away from home, except a body turned up in a building that used to be owned by her father."

"So, you want to know if the girl really ran away or perhaps if she didn't get very far away from home?"

"Yes. I would also like you to check into the father, the brother, and there was also a sister named Harriet, maybe from Boca Raton or Fort Lauderdale."

"Do you want financials, too?" he asked. "It might take a little longer if you need that."

"Yes, please include financials." The possibility of Albert or Harry in financial trouble had crossed her mind a couple of times.

"What's the time line?" he asked. "How recent is this?"

"Not very. It was in 1978. For the missing person check, I think December 1978 until January 1980. While you're at it, check for all blonde, seventeen to twenty-four-year-olds who disappeared during this time frame."

"1978?" He snorted. "Are you kidding me? That's forty years ago."

"I know. I did the math. But, the building has been occupied since February 1980, after being empty for more than a year. We know when Annaliese disappeared, but if it's not her, then it's someone else who got themselves stashed into the wall."

"Jeez, Red." Ray Ban paused, and she heard him sigh. "What kind of place are you living in? I've talked to you more in the last three months than I did in the whole three years prior."

He had provided Libby with information about the smuggling and money laundering scheme she had uncovered the previous August.

"It's actually a very nice little beach town."

She heard a harrumph before he said, "I'll be in touch."

The line went dead. She took another long drink of beer.

Chapter 8

Mid-morning, Thanksgiving Day, Mariposa Beach
Scones, Pies and a Drive-by

"Good morning." Ida opened her door to Libby, who had a paper bag and two cups of coffee in a carrier.

"I brought your favorite orange scones and a mocha latte."

"Thank you. Come in."

The living room was one large room that included the dining area opposite the front door. Ida's walker was tucked in by the sofa near the front door. She could maneuver well throughout her home without it.

Libby noticed the photos were pushed to one side of the table, leaving room for one place setting.

"Push those aside and make room to sit down. I'll get some plates."

Libby gently moved three stacks of photos, trying to keep them just as Ida had stacked them. Ida returned with plates, and Libby placed the coffee in front of her.

"Happy Thanksgiving," Libby said, holding up her cup.

Ida touched her cup to Libby's and nodded. "Happy Thanksgiving." She took a sip. "Are you going to Julia's today?"

"Yes, I'm responsible for the pies. Well, not directly responsible. Louisa baked them."

"I appreciate the scones." Ida took a bite and another sip of coffee.

"How are you doing?" Libby asked.

"All right. I've been sorting through all this stuff."

"Did you find anything?"

"Perhaps." Ida leaned towards her. "I found an old address book. I'm waiting for some people to call me back."

"Who did you call?" Libby asked.

Zsa Zsa was sniffing around Ida's chair, hoping for a crumb. "No, baby girl."

Zsa Zsa sat to attention. Ida laughed and rubbed behind her ears. "I called some old contacts hoping to find out about the building, rumors about Albert and who he was paying hush money to, who he was fooling around with…anything I could think of to ask."

"What have you found out?"

"A lot of time has passed, people got married and had kids, and their kids had kids, and we live our lives, and if we're lucky, we got old."

"So, nothing specific?"

"I found the name of a contractor in Sid's address book. The company is still open, but the original owner sold it. He said that Buddy, that's his name, is still around and lives on a boat in the marina. He's going to get his number and call me back."

"That's great news! Do you think this guy might be the contractor who worked on that building?"

"Perhaps. I hope he calls back tomorrow."

"Ida, you're becoming quite the little investigator."

Ida laughed so loud Zsa Zsa jumped up from her spot on the sofa and started barking. "Zsa Zsa, shhh."

"You said that the family home was sold after Albert died."

"The house sold at auction about twenty years ago after Albert died. Albert was always in debt. Sell one thing to finance another. Good thing the Board ran the company." She took a sip of coffee, then continued, "Sid stayed on with the company after Albert died, but he didn't last too long after that, my Sid. He told me stuff that he probably shouldn't have, but I never told anyone what we talked about. You know, what happens in the bedroom, stays in the bedroom."

"What did Sid tell you?" Libby asked with a smile.

"Albert sold the hotel to finance the supermarket. Over the years, he sold most of the land, too. That house used to sit on more than fifty acres, but by the time he died, all the land he had left was the plot the house sits on today."

"What about the brother and sister? Did they have any stake in the house and grounds?"

"I think Albert must have bought them out when his mother died. Sid told me that Harry hated that house and never would have wanted to live there anyway."

"Do you know who bought the house?" Libby asked.

"No, but they've fixed it up nice."

The well-landscaped, two-story brick house stood off the beach road behind an ornate, black iron gate.

"I'm going to see if I can look it up in the court records. Find out if the people who bought the house had any connection to Albert and the family." Libby finished her coffee, then picked up the plates and took them into the kitchen.

"Thanks, again for the coffee and scones," Ida said.

"Do you want to come to Julia's for dinner?" Libby asked. "My mother is in town, and I know she'd love to meet you."

"Thank you, but no. Etta and I are going to The Jetty for their Thanksgiving Day special dinner. We're going to do the Uber. Etta has it on her phone."

The Jetty was the fanciest restaurant in town.

"That sounds wonderful."

"Are you going to see Jack?"

"I don't know. I hope so. Jack wants to see his father, but he's also on-call today."

"Hopefully, no one gets shot, stabbed, burglared, assaulted, or any other manner of mayhem that would call him out." Ida stood and walked with Libby to the front door.

"I hope you and Etta have a wonderful dinner and Uber adventure."

• • •

An hour later, Libby pulled out of her driveway, pumpkin, apple and chocolate meringue pies safely enclosed within carriers on the floorboard. Instead of turning left to take the most direct route, she decided to turn right and take the two-lane beach road past the old Hobson House. Before leaving, she'd done a quick computer search of the online county property records but didn't have much luck. Once she was sure she had the correct address, she would call Ray Ban again.

She turned right onto Beach Road. It ran parallel to the Gulf of Mexico until it turned to meet the main road to Sarasota. The old Hobson House sat halfway between Libby's street and the turn off to the main road.

Libby stopped at a beach pull off just past the house. For a better view, she walked back to stand directly across the street, her back to the water. The double iron gate was at least ten feet tall, and, from where she stood, there appeared to be a call box on the left hand side. Beyond the gate, the driveway wound past the front door and curved around the house to a garage to the back on the left side. Behind her was a wooden walkway down to the beach.

The beach probably belongs to them, too.

Libby unfolded the copy of the photograph of Annaliese standing in front of the house. Forty years ago, there was no fancy iron gate, that Libby could see, and the driveway was crushed shell and not decorative concrete.

A lot changes in forty years. Hell, your life can change from one moment to the next.

She snapped a couple of photos with her phone and returned to her car.

• • •

Libby arrived at Julia's condo on Longboat Key, a long barrier island off the coast of Sarasota, with pies in hand.

"Mary Beth, I'm so happy to see you."

Libby's mother, Helen O'Brien, had a hard time calling Libby by her chosen name. When Libby moved to Florida, she wanted a new start and didn't want her old life to find her so easily. Mary Elizabeth O'Brien became Libby Marshall. Libby was a nickname her grandmother used to call her, and she'd gotten used to being called by that name. Mary Beth seemed childish, like something shed or put aside with maturity.

Libby returned her mother's hug. "Mom, I'm so happy you were able to come down."

David rescued the pies. "Don't drop the pies." He kissed Libby's cheek and placed the pie carriers on the kitchen counter.

"You're late," Julia called from the dining room. "We were getting ready to carve the turkey."

Libby followed Julia's voice into the open dining and living room. "Sorry. I stopped by Ida's to check on her."

"How is she?" Julia asked. "You should have invited her."

"I did, but she has an Uber adventure with Etta planned for dinner at The Jetty."

Julia's condo had an open floor plan that provided a wide angle view of the Gulf of Mexico from her living room and dining room. "What a beautiful day. I never tire of the view from your condo, Aunt Julia."

"God bless Harry Gordon for purchasing this condo when he retired."

Harry Gordon was Julia's second husband, who died several years ago.

"Dinner is on the table," Helen said.

Once they were seated, Julia said, "I am so thankful to have my whole family here with me to share the bounty of this meal."

"Let's eat before we get too mushy," David said as he stood to carve the turkey.

"The meal is quite bountiful," Libby said. "You have enough here to serve three times the people."

"We'll have plenty of leftovers," Helen said.

Once their plates were full, there was silence as they all tasted the food and then gave compliments to the cooks.

"Mar...Libby," Helen began, "How is Ida? You said you stopped to see her on your way here."

"She's had a rough week. I wanted to make sure she wasn't spending Thanksgiving alone."

"David told us about the discovery of the skeleton in the wall of Eleanor's old shop," Julia said between bites of turkey.

"A skeleton?" Helen asked.

"Yes, it has been in that wall for forty years, and Ida thinks she knows who she was." Libby cut the slice of turkey on her plate. "Dinner is delicious, Julia."

"And you discovered it?" Helen asked.

"Well, not by myself. I was helping a friend remove the drywall."

"I think that space will make a great gallery," David said.

Libby nodded in gratitude for the subject change. "I dropped your name about music for the gallery opening. Steve Devereaux should be giving you a call." Libby turned to David, who was sitting next to her. "I was thinking about that student of yours, the harpist."

David taught at the local school for the creative and performing arts.

"That's an excellent idea! I'll talk to her on Monday."

"I was hoping your young man would be here today. I'm looking forward to meeting him." Helen took a sip of wine and looked over her glass at her daughter.

"He went to see his father out in Arcadia. It's east of here. He's a detective with the Sheriff's Office, and he's on-call today."

"That's the thing about life with a detective. It's hard to plan something or have a nice dinner with family. Something always comes up." Helen finished her wine. "You should remember all the dinners your father missed."

"Jack's a great guy," David said.

"He really is a nice guy." Julia poured wine into Helen's glass.

"What about that rule you had about not dating policeman and lawyers?" Helen asked.

"I still don't date lawyers," Libby quipped.

Chapter 9

Black Friday

Like any other American town, Black Friday was a busy retail day for Mariposa Beach. Libby, Mimi and Mimi's husband Paul were up early decorating the café and helping the other shopkeepers in the courtyard with decorations in preparation for the traditional Christmas holiday kick-off.

Mimi loved decorating for every holiday, but Christmas was her favorite. She touched off the decorations by hanging a crystal mistletoe ornament over the saloon doors between the kitchen and café as well as over the hallway entry leading to the café's public restrooms and a few other locations throughout the café. She even shared a few with the other shopkeepers around the courtyard.

The café was busy with holiday shoppers out for breakfast, brunch and lunch – before, during and after shopping. In the courtyard, Libby's cousin, David, and their friend, Ben, were playing guitars and singing seasonal favorites and audience requests.

Libby crossed the courtyard while the guys were singing "Let it Snow." She laughed as the weather was a balmy seventy-eight degrees. At the end of the song, the guys burst out laughing, too.

They've had too many mimosas already this morning.

Libby opened the door of The Mariposa Mystic to the exotic scent of incense permeating the air of the small shop. There was a display of candles, incense and incense burners in the front of the store with a bookshelf on the right that held Tarot cards and books on Tarot, spirit animals, self-help and other subjects. The cashier stand was in the middle of the store on the right, and a familiar, crystal mistletoe ornament was attached to the top of a bookshelf behind it.

Rachel was behind the desk, ringing up a customer. Steve was standing in front of the crystals and stones, talking to a young woman with merchandise in her hands.

"Thank you so much." Rachel handed her customer a bag decorated with fairies.

"What a cute shop," said the customer, a woman, about forty, wearing shorts and a T-shirt with a palm tree lit with Christmas lights.

"Thank you."

Libby stepped up to the desk as the customer moved away. "Looks like your opening day is a hit."

"She's been busy since the moment she opened," Steve said. "She hasn't even stopped for lunch."

"That's one of the reasons I'm here," Libby said. "I've been watching people popping in and out all morning and thought I would ask if you wanted me to bring you a turkey sandwich."

"That would be wonderful," Rachel said, as another customer appeared at the desk holding a necklace with a beautiful Larimar stone.

Steve followed Libby out of the store. "If I have half the crowd at my opening that she's had today, I'll be a happy man."

"I saw this morning's paper," Libby said. "I think that spread will be good for your launch. A haunted art gallery has a nice ring to it."

"Kenji tipped off the papers," Steve said. "I didn't know he did that until the reporter showed up at my door."

As they crossed the courtyard, David and Ben were leading the customers sitting at the café's tables in a rousing rendition of "Walking in a Winter Wonderland."

"Excuse me, are you Steve Devereaux?"

Steve and Libby turned to a woman with short dark hair speckled with gray and pale blue eyes behind bright red glasses.

"Yes, ma'am. How can I help you?"

"I saw this morning's paper." She held up the paper and pointed to the picture of Steve in front of the wall. "I'm Margaret Hobson Blanchard, Annaliese's cousin."

Libby and Steve exchanged glances.

"Please come in," Libby said.

Libby led Steve and Margaret into the café, seated them at an open table and said she would bring them iced teas. Mimi was behind the counter, and Libby asked her to make Rachel's sandwich order.

"Who is that with Steve?" Mimi asked.

"That's Annaliese's cousin!" Libby poured three glasses of iced tea and placed three Christmas tree cookies on a plate.

"The skeleton girl?!"

"Yes, she saw the newspaper article and just showed up."

Libby brought the iced teas to the table as Margaret asked, "Was that body Annaliese?"

"The police are trying to figure that out. In fact, would you be open to giving a DNA sample?" Libby asked. "It might be helpful in identifying if it is Annaliese or someone else."

"Of course, I will. That's one of the reasons I decided to drive down to see you." She took a sip of tea.

"So you live around here?" Steve asked.

"Yes. In Parrish," she said, indicating a town about an hour to the north of Mariposa Beach. "I couldn't believe my eyes when I opened this morning's paper to see this story." She unfolded the paper again to the photograph of Steve in front of the gallery. "Was she really in the wall of the old store?"

"Yes, I'm sorry, she was," Libby said.

"We were pulling down the old closet and ended up finding a false wall, and she was in there," Steve said.

"Ida Sullivan had a photo of your family at a garden party just before Christmas in 1978," Libby said.

Margaret wore a cross-body shoulder bag. She slowly unzipped it and pulled out a copy of the same photo they'd seen at Ida's house.

"My mother had a copy of this photo. Sid Sullivan must have given it to my parents." She pointed to a girl about twelve years old. "That's me."

"Do you remember what happened that day?" Libby asked.

"Not really. I was only twelve. So Annaliese argued with her Dad. Don't all teenagers argue with their parents?"

"I sure did," Steve said.

"Did you see much of what happened that day?" Libby asked.

"Not really." Margaret Hobson Blanchard paused, took a deep breath and shook her head.

"Mrs. Blanchard, are you all right?" Steve asked.

"Perhaps it's a bit creepy, but I'd like to see…to see where she was."

Steve looked across the table at Libby and shrugged his shoulders. "Of course, I'm happy to show you, but we've pulled the whole wall down, so you won't see the compartment where she was…uh…left."

"When my father was dying, I took care of him. As he got closer to the end, he started to see things. One night, he was particularly agitated. He thought he wouldn't get into heaven because of this terrible thing. He swore it wasn't his fault, that he didn't do it. It was an accident. He said he was sorry, but he had to help his brother. He kept saying it over and over. 'I did a very bad thing. I'm sorry.'"

"When was this, Mrs. Blanchard?" Libby asked.

"Please call me Margaret." She paused and took another deep breath. "My father passed four years ago."

"What 'bad thing' do you think he meant?" Libby asked.

"I think he helped Uncle Albert clean up a mess of some kind. He kept muttering that it was Albert's fault and what else could he have done. It was awful to hear him crying. I didn't want him to have such an agonizing passing. He was so upset. I thought he was having hallucinations, but when I saw this newspaper article, it seemed to make sense."

"So, you're worried that your uncle killed her and your father helped him cover it up?"

"I know I'm probably jumping to conclusions, but my father was so upset and afraid and now this." She ran her hand over the picture in the newspaper.

"Can you remember anything that your uncle might have done, or did you hear any weird rumors?" Libby pressed on. "I know you were a kid, but sometimes kids overhear stuff."

"As I got older, I realized that Uncle Albert was a sleezeball. There were rumors that he had affairs and paid hush money all over town." She shrugged. "I graduated and went off to college, and that was that."

• • •

A few minutes later, they stood in Steve's gallery in front of the wall. Jack had called Steve that morning and gave him clearance to resume renovations. So, before going to help Rachel in her shop, Steve had knocked down the remainder of the framing boards and was in the process of cleaning the brick.

"I thought she ran away," Margaret said. "That's what Uncle Albert told everyone."

"That's what Ida Sullivan said, too," Libby added.

Steve and Libby watched as Margaret walked around the room.

"I live across the street from her," Libby said, trying to keep the conversation much lighter than what had happened in the space they were in.

"I always liked her. Do you think it would be all right if I stopped by her house?"

"I'm sure she'd be happy to see you."

Margaret walked to the back door, arms crossed over her chest and looked outside to the parking lot. "Once, years ago, I came to the gift shop that was here. Curiosity, I guess. I hadn't been in the building since I was a small child." She returned to the center of the room where Steve and Libby were standing. "And all along she was right here."

"Yes, ma'am. She was," Steve said.

"Thank you for showing me."

"If you should think of anything else or if any of your siblings should remember anything, please give me a call at the café."

"Who should I contact about the DNA sample, and how do I get to Ida's house?"

Libby gave her Jack's phone number, directions to Ida's house, thanked her and wished her well. From the gallery door, they watched her walk back to her car parked on the street in front of the café.

"It must have been painful to hear that from her dad's deathbed," Steve said. "Do you think he got absolution?"

"I don't know." Libby turned to face him. "But I do hope there is a special place in hell for people like Albert who take advantage of someone weaker and do something like this." She gestured toward the wall.

Chapter 10

Late Monday Afternoon
Smudge

Libby, Mimi, Rachel and Steve stood in the middle of the gallery, facing the exposed brick wall. Almost all of the drywall had been removed, leaving only the wood frame of the false wall and the exposed brick. Although Steve had resumed his renovations upon Jack's clearance of the crime scene, Rachel insisted on cleansing the space before he disturbed the girl's final resting place any further.

It was late afternoon, and the light was dim. The only natural light came from the two large display windows and French doors that faced the street and the small windows in the back door. A night light burning in the office to the right of the back door cast an amber shadow into the room.

Rachel removed her bag from her shoulder and set it on the table. The bag was dark brown, well-worn leather with long fringe and a flap like a messenger bag. It reminded Libby of an old leather purse of her mother's she had found in their attic. A leftover from her hippie-boho teenage years, her mother had called it.

They watched as Rachel began to remove items from the bag. Mimi was at her side, captivated as Rachel assembled her implements, like a surgeon setting up for a procedure. Steve and Libby observed from their place in the middle of the room.

"Do you believe in this stuff?" Steve asked.

"The jury is out on that one," Libby said. "But it can't hurt."

"Did you smudge the café?"

"Yes. Mimi insisted," Libby said, leaning towards him, speaking in funereal tones. "The café was a tavern with quite the checkered past. She wanted no left over bad mojo. If you believe in that sort of thing, of course."

Rachel removed a bowl-shaped shell from her bag and set it in front of her. Next to that, she placed two small packages of herbs, a box of kitchen matches and a large feather that was bright royal blue along one side tinged with shiny black throughout.

"What kind of shell is that?" Mimi asked.

"It's abalone." Rachel picked up the herbs. "This is sage and lavender. I'm going to use them to create our smudge." She opened the sage package, poured about two tablespoons into the palm of her hand, and then crushed it between her fingers into the bowl of the shell. Then she did the same with a smaller amount of lavender. She rubbed her hands together as she explained, "The sage will drive out any negative energies, and the lavender will restore balance and help bring peace to this space."

Steve raised his eyebrows to Libby, who shrugged. Mimi was absorbing every word and action.

"Steve," Rachel said, bringing him abruptly to attention.

"Yes."

Rachel turned to face them. "Before we get started, can you please open the windows?"

"I'm not sure if I can." He checked the storefront windows to discover they were sealed shut, so he opened one side of the French doors.

"I'll get the back door," Libby said.

Once finished with their tasks, they returned to the center of the room. Rachel asked Mimi if she would like to light the smudge. Mimi's crystal blue eyes grew wide as she met Rachel's encouraging gaze. As Mimi removed a match and struck it against the side of the box, Libby detected a slight tremor. The strike pierced the silence like an exploding lightbulb.

"Light the sage," Rachel directed, nodding toward the shell.

Mimi set the box on the table and slid the lit match to the edge of the shell. The fire engulfed the herbs, and Mimi instinctively stepped back and shook out the match. Rachel blew out the flames and allowed the herbs to smolder, gray smoke rising out of the bowl.

With the shell in her left hand and the feather in her right, Rachel turned toward the northeastern corner where the brick wall met the front wall by the display window.

In a low soothing voice, she said, "I'm asking Spirit to bring the guides and angels into this space to cleanse it of all negativity and replace it with positivity. To bring in light and love. To cleanse and purify. To push out the old and bring in the new. To fill this space with light and love."

She used the feather to waft the smoke into space. The pungent scent invaded Libby's nostrils and filled her sinuses. A cross breeze through the open doors dispersed the smoke, surrounding them in a mysterious haze.

Rachel slowly moved clockwise along the brick wall, continuously moving the feather to send the smoke upwards and around them. As she moved closer to the framed-in compartment where the body had been entombed, the wind picked up, blowing Libby's red curls into her face. The back door slammed shut, and the three, now huddled together, jumped in unison. Simultaneously, Steve grabbed Libby's arm, Libby grabbed Mimi's arm and Mimi gasped, her hands moving to her heart. Rachel remained calm and asked Spirit to bring in love and light.

As Rachel moved in front of the girl's resting place, Steve, Libby and Mimi were still holding onto each other. Rachel halted in front of where the compartment had been, holding the feather in the air. She dropped her head as if in prayer and then turned her gaze to the ceiling.

There was a flickering of light in the back of the room. All four of them turned. The flickering continued, alternately casting them from almost total darkness to the amber tinge of light in the back corner of the room.

"What's that?" Mimi's voice shook as she asked aloud what Libby was silently wondering.

Libby felt Steve's grip on her arm tighten.

"The night light in the office," he whispered. "There must be a short or something."

Rachel turned to face them. Her brown eyes glistened as she spoke. "A young woman in her early twenties or so has presented herself to me."

Libby took in a breath as she and her companions held onto each other. Libby knew Rachel was intuitive. Rachel read Tarot cards in the café and now in her new shop. When asked, she openly offered her interpretations and impressions of people and situations. She was usually correct in those interpretations. She had mentioned that occasionally spirits speak to her, but Libby had never been present during an active conversation.

"She has long blonde hair and eyes the color of blue topaz."

"Anneliese?" Libby asked.

"She is shaking her head 'no,'" Rachel said, staring over Libby's shoulder.

"Then, who?" Libby glanced backwards.

"She is showing me a dove," Rachel said. "That means she is at peace." Rachel paused for a moment. Then she turned back to the wall and continued with the cleansing. When she reached the southeast corner, she stopped.

The three in the middle of the room had loosened their grips on each other and turned slightly to watch Rachel as she continued her smudge.

"She bears no ill will to anyone. She is truly at peace. She knows her death was an accident. The person did not mean to kill her."

Rachel continued moving clockwise. Libby looked from Steve to Mimi.

"This is amazing," Mimi said.

"I can't believe I'm standing here watching this," Steve said.

"It's not Annaliese, and it was an accident?" Libby asked.

Rachel finished her smudge where she started, making a complete clockwise rotation of the room. In the end, she took a deep breath and placed her shell and feather on the table. She looked exhausted. Steve offered her a chair.

"This takes a lot out of me." Rachel sank into the wooden chair.

Steve stood next to her, his hand on her shoulder.

"Was there any indication as to her identity?" Libby asked.

"No, she only indicated that she is not Annaliese."

Rachel rubbed her head and closed her eyes.

"Anything else?" Libby asked.

"Libby, this isn't an interrogation," Mimi said.

"Yes, of course, I'm sorry. I can get carried away sometimes." Libby stepped back, hands in the air.

"There is one other thing," Rachel said, opening her eyes and looking up at Libby and Mimi and then over her shoulder to Steve.

"And?" Libby asked.

"There was a child, a baby," Rachel said.

"Do you mean with her?" Steve asked. "Did they kill a child, too?"

"How could someone kill a child and stuff them in a wall? It's bad enough to do that to an adult, but a child?" Mimi was close to tears.

"No-no. That's not what I'm saying," Rachel said.

"She was pregnant," Libby said, barely above a whisper. "Is that what you're saying?"

Rachel nodded. "Yes, this girl was pregnant. I could see the baby inside of her. She was holding a dove in one hand and her belly in the other."

• • •

Later that evening, Libby sat in her living room, a drink in hand, trying to process what had happened that afternoon. Steve had said he would escort Rachel home once she was feeling better. Libby and Mimi had walked back to the café in silence. In pure Mimi form, the only thing she said was that she thought Steve and Rachel had some kind chemistry-thing going on. They closed the café, and went home to process the day's events in their own way.

There was a knock at the door, and Jack poked his head inside.

"Are you here?"

Libby laid her head on the back of the sofa and called over her shoulder to him in the kitchen behind her. "Yes, in the living room."

He shut the door, and as he came into the room, he leaned over the sofa and kissed her neck.

"Bad day?" he asked. "You're sitting here in the dark with a drink." He came around and sat next to her on the sofa.

"It was an interesting one," she said, taking a sip of her drink and then offering him the glass.

He took a sip and handed it back to her. "A tequila day, huh?"

A beer day was a typical, good day, a wine day was a better day, but a tequila day was either a bad day or a day that required serious contemplation.

She smiled and finished the glass, impressed that Jack knew her so well. It felt so good that he knew the tequila meant she'd had a rough one.

"Do you want to tell me now or over dinner?"

She turned to face him and kissed him on the lips. "Now."

She told him what happened at the gallery in great detail. She watched his face as she revealed that the girl was not Annaliese.

"Did you know that she wasn't Annaliese?" she asked.

"I received Mrs. Blanchard's results."

"That was fast, especially on a holiday weekend."

"I have connections."

"And?" she asked.

"Mrs. Blanchard is 99.9% *not* related to the body in the wall."

"So, she isn't Annaliese." Libby sighed and leaned back against the sofa.

"The answer is no. Mrs. Blanchard and the person in the wall are not blood relatives."

"There was something else that Rachel said today that has me a little bit…" She took a deep breath. "Tequila day."

Jack leaned back against the sofa and turned to meet her gaze. "What did she say?"

"Rachel said that there was a baby. The girl was pregnant."

"Pregnant?"

"Did the autopsy say anything like that?"

He turned away and closed his eyes for a moment. When he opened them, she was watching him. He leaned forward and took her hands in his. She sat up and turned to face him. "There were a few, small, extra bones that would seem to indicate that the girl was possibly pregnant at the time of death."

Libby dropped his hands, turned and covered her face with her hands. He put his arms around her, kissed the top of her head and held her tight until she raised her head.

"I'm sorry," she said. "I don't know what's come over me."

He smiled and kissed her temple. "I have been at a cleansing before. My mother did them. Those sessions can bring up lots of emotions and feelings."

"I had such a sense of loss. It reminded me of how I felt when I had the miscarriage."

"Feel better now?"

She nodded. "Yes, I do. Thank you for being here." She laid back onto his chest. She felt safe in his arms. This was where she belonged.

"My pleasure."

She sat up. His eyes searched her face. He was still worried, she thought. "All this feeling has made me hungry. Do you want to go to the Veranda Bar for some shrimp?" She stood and went to the mirror behind the sofa.

"Yes, I'm starving. I thought you'd never ask."

"Oh, by the way, there's one more thing," she said, watching him in the mirror as she fluffed her hair.

"What's that?"

"It was an accident."

"What was an accident?" He met her eyes in the mirror.

"The girl said that she is at peace with what happened because she knows it was an accident."

"So, does she want to solve this case and identify who shot her in the head by accident?"

"I don't know. Rachel only called him 'the person.'"

"Perhaps Rachel could call her back and ask for more details," Jack said, opening the back door.

"I don't think it works that way."

"Of course it doesn't." Jack followed her out the door and closed it behind them.

Chapter 11

A Few Days Later – Early December The List Narrows

Libby sat on the picnic table near the concession area at the beach two blocks from the cafe. Since her first visit to Mariposa Beach nearly four years ago, this spot had been her special place where she came to think, listen to waves crashing on the beach, to people watch or marvel in the beauty of a sunset.

She couldn't get the dead girl and baby out of her mind. She wondered who the girl was and how she ended up in that wall. Where was she killed? Why and when was she moved? Who killed her? Did the father of the baby do it? Considering what Margaret Blanchard said about her father, Libby suspected that he helped his brother move the body to the empty building. Perhaps they were the ones who entombed her in that wall. Since she definitely was not Annaliese, where did Annaliese go and where had she been for the last forty years?

It was a chilly afternoon, and there weren't many people at the beach. The wind picked up, and Libby wrapped her sweater around her body and folded her arms over her chest.

The Christmas lights on the concession building flashed on and began to twinkle. Since moving from Ohio, Christmas lights on palm trees and inflatable Santas amid tropical foliage seemed foreign to her, but she was getting used to it. She was surprised to realize that she liked the quirkiness of a Florida Christmas.

"I thought I would find you here."

Libby immediately recognized the voice. She turned and greeted her cousin with a huge smile. "David, hello."

He stepped up onto the bench and sat next to her on the picnic table.

"A chilly afternoon, isn't it?" He zipped his jacket and hunched his back against the wind.

"Feels good," she said.

"That was sort of a weird Thanksgiving." David bumped her shoulder. "You all right?"

"Of course, I'm fine. I know my mother is just looking out for me and is worried that what happened with my father being killed on the job, could also happen to me if I continue this relationship with Jack."

"I think Jack is good for you. You seem more yourself, or should I say, more the old you since you started seeing him."

"I feel more myself than I have in a very long time."

David put his arm around Libby and pulled her close. "I'm so glad."

Libby squeezed him and then pulled out of his embrace, "Did Steve talk to you about music for the gallery opening?"

"Yes, he did. I do have a harpist who can play during the cocktail hour. This will be a great experience for her since it will be a smaller group and not necessarily on a stage. She has a little bit of stage fright."

David was an advocate of providing his students with as many performing opportunities as possible.

"Thanks. I knew you would come through."

"Since Ben and I are playing the New Year's Eve Party at the Inn, I asked Ben to come to the opening. We can sing a few Christmas carols, and I was hoping you would join us in a mix up of "Silent Night" and "O Holy Night. Remember we did that a few years ago at one of Mom's parties."

"I would love to, but I don't think I could play any instrument. My hand is not quite back to normal, even with therapy and squeezing that stress ball." Libby opened her right hand, moved her fingers and then clenched them into a fist. "Almost, but not quite where it was."

"No worries, just bring your voice. There's nothing wrong with that."

• • •

David walked with Libby back to the café. He picked up a coffee to go and said he needed to meet Ben to rehearse for the New Year's Eve show. Libby picked up a cleaning cloth and started to wipe down the counter. She was finishing the display case when her phone buzzed.

"Ray Ban?"

"Hey, Red. You sure love to challenge me."

"What did you find out?" She stopped, cleaning cloth in hand.

"After checking, double checking and elimination of those that didn't meet the criteria, i.e., not the right dates, age range or race, hair color, etc., I've narrowed it down to four possibilities."

"Four…that's not too bad," she said. "Though, sadly, four young women disappeared within that time frame between early 1978 and late 1979.

"I'll send you the info via e-mail tonight. I'm still compiling what I've got, which is not a lot compared to what is available today. There's still lots of information that has not yet been digitized, as you know. So, I've identified those in my report. You'll have to check those out yourself."

"Thanks. I owe you."

"I'll put it on your tab."

And he was gone.

• • •

Later that evening, propped up with her laptop against the pillows in her bed, Libby paged through the information Ray Ban had sent her.

"Jeanette McDonald from Ft. Myers, Lynette Watkins from Tampa, Georgia Nielsen from Venice and Melanie Cooper from LaBelle." She read the names aloud while sipping on white wine and thumbing through high school yearbook photos and newspaper clippings on her laptop screen.

Ray Ban was right; the information is scarce.

One news report caught her eye, though. Melanie Cooper from LaBelle had a job working at Hobson's in Mariposa Beach. Her senior picture from the LaBelle High School yearbook revealed a pretty blonde with a sweet smile, and she looked quite a bit like Annaliese Hobson.

A thought crossed Libby's mind, and she pulled Ida's photo that she had copied out of the back of the legal pad on which she had drawn her time line. There was a server in the picture that looked like a girl with a long blonde ponytail.

The background was too grainy, and the girl was too far in the background to be sure, but it was a possibility.

The phone buzzed, and she jumped.

"Hi, Jack."

"What are you up to this evening?"

She shut her laptop, picked up the remote and turned on the television. "Just sitting on the bed, watching some TV, having a little white wine."

"I wish I was there with you."

Libby moved the laptop to the side and relaxed into the pillows. "Me, too."

"The Sarasota Boat Parade is next weekend. Have you ever been to a boat parade?"

"No, but I've seen the boats at the Paradise Park Marina decorated for the holidays."

"That doesn't count. Do you want to have some dinner and watch the boat parade? We can walk to a good viewing spot from my place."

"I'm looking forward to seeing your new place. From what you've told me, it sounds wonderful."

Jack had recently moved to a guest house on Bird Key, an island community just across the bay from Downtown Sarasota. He had solved a robbery for the owners of the house. They became friends and offered Jack a place to live, with the thought that having a police detective living on the property would deter any future problems.

He had been living with his brother, Dr. Mike Seiler, for almost six years, after splitting with his ex-wife. His brother and his girlfriend, a nurse, were getting serious and talking about marriage, so Jack decided it was a good time to take his friends up on their offer to live in their guest house.

"My place isn't much. It's a tiny, one-bedroom guest house. It's not even really my place. I'm doing a favor for a friend."

"I'm looking forward to the boat parade and seeing your little place on the bay."

"Bring an overnight bag."

Chapter 12

A Few Days Later
Follow the Lead

Ida Sullivan called the café just after the lunch rush. When Mimi answered the phone, she asked for Libby.

"Ida, are you all right?" Mimi asked.

"I need to talk to Libby about…you know." Ida whispered the last part.

Mimi rolled her eyes and held out the phone to Libby who was cleaning tables and carrying a tray of dirty dishes and table trash. "It's Ida. She wants to talk to you about the skeleton in the wall."

"I heard that." Ida's voice carried through the receiver. "You don't have to blab it all over the place."

Libby reached for the phone and mouthed "What?" to Mimi, who rolled her eyes, shrugged and took the tray from her.

"Ida, is everything all right?" Libby could hear Zsa Zsa barking, then Ida covered the phone to shush the dog.

"I need you to come over here as soon as you can. I got a call back. We need to track down this lead." She was talking fast, excitement filling her voice.

"Whoa, there," Libby said. "What do you mean 'track down a lead'?"

"I have the address of that contractor. We can take a little drive and see what we see. He lives on a boat at the marina."

"Just a drive?" Libby asked.

"Maybe we'll get out and take a little look around." Her suggestion rang with anticipation and even more excitement.

"Let me check with Mimi and Louisa. I'll be there at two o'clock unless I call back to set another time."

"Wonderful. See you then."

Libby thought sure she heard a little giggle before she disconnected.

● ● ●

Libby pulled into Ida's driveway only a few minutes after the agreed upon time. Ida must have been watching at the window because she was out the door, pushing her walker, before Libby could open the car door. Libby was surprised to see Fletcher Smith close behind her. Zsa Zsa was barking at them from her spot in the front window.

"I'll sit in the back," Ida said.

Libby hit the button to open the SUV's lift gate and headed towards the back of the vehicle. Fletcher folded Ida's walker and placed it in the cargo space.

"What's going on?" she asked.

"I offered to go along for the ride. I hope that's all right."

Before Libby could utter, "Of course not," there was a beep behind them. They turned to see Strauss in his red Mercedes convertible with a live Christmas tree in the back seat. With the front seat pushed as far forward as possible, the tree was tied to the car in all directions, to anything that would support a tie-down.

"That's a nice tree you have there," Fletcher said.

"Brigitte wanted a live tree this year," Strauss said. "Where are you three going?"

"We're taking Ida on a short errand," Fletcher said. "Her walker doesn't fit in my car, so Libby offered to drive."

"You guys and your small sporty cars. Don't drive too fast, or you'll lose your tree."

Libby could feel Strauss' gaze on her. She turned to check on Ida who was waving at Strauss from the back seat of the car.

"That tree is bigger than your car," Ida hollered.

"I should be getting this home. I had to make two trips. Brigitte was first." Strauss tipped his driving cap, put the car in gear and drove off down the street.

"He'd better get home," Fletcher said and laughed, as Libby closed the lift gate. "I wouldn't want to leave Brigitte waiting. She's quite scary, a real badass."

Once inside the car, Libby turned to Ida and said, "Where are we going?"

Ida handed her a piece of paper with the address of Paradise Park Marina, slip number forty-seven.

"Who is this?" She dropped the paper into the cup holder.

"He's the contractor who did some work for Hobson's, including, I think, the building where you all found whoever she is."

Libby had informed Ida of the DNA results the day after Jack told her.

"He may not have done the work, but he might remember who did," Fletcher said.

"Okay, we'll go check it out. Just surveillance for now," Libby said.

"I think we should at least talk to the guy," Ida said. "That's why I asked Fletcher. He has experience with enhanced interrogation methods."

"What?!" Libby asked. "We aren't going to water board anybody. Are we?"

Fletcher laughed. "Don't you remember? I used to be a fraud investigator. I'm a certified interviewer."

"We're certified, all right," Libby muttered, as she turned to back the car out of the driveway.

• • •

A few minutes later, Libby turned into the Paradise Park Marina. The road wound through a small park with a paved walking path and playground before ending at the marina. Libby pulled into a spot that faced the water. Fletcher retrieved Ida's walker from the cargo area and opened it up.

"Which way?" she asked.

"This way," Libby said. "The numbers are on the side."

They located the slip, which was at the end of the row.

"Ida, are you sure this walkway is stable enough to walk down to the boat?" Libby asked.

"Yes, I'm fine."

"I could go down and see if the guy is there," Fletcher offered.

"No, I'm going down there, too," Ida insisted. "I'll walk slow and be careful." She pushed her walker onto the floating pier.

Libby and Fletcher exchanged a glance and followed her.

The wooden pier was wide enough to push her walker with plenty of space on either side as well as a railing that ran along the right side. There were three boats on the right and a couple of empty slips on the left.

"It appears to be this one coming up here," Fletcher said, pointing to an older cabin cruiser to the right. It was white with Lilly Belle painted on the side in an elegant red script.

"Ahoy there on the Lilly Belle," Fletcher called out.

"Ahoy?" Ida asked. "You sound like a damn pirate."

"Isn't that how you call to someone on a boat?" Fletcher held up his hands and looked at Libby for validation.

"I don't know." Libby said, stifling a laugh.

"Hey, whaddaya want?"

The three on the pier looked up into the grizzled, unshaven face of a man who Libby estimated to be about sixty. He wore cutoff jeans and a pocket T-shirt. He appeared as if he had just fallen out of bed.

"Are you Buddy?" Ida asked.

"Who's askin'?"

"I'm Ida Sullivan. This is Libby and Fletcher. My husband used to work for the Hobson's."

"So, a lot of people worked for the Hobson's, back in the day." Buddy rubbed his hands over his stubbly face. He was lean with skinny arms and legs but had a little beer belly protruding under his shirt.

"We're sorry to bother you, Mr. uh…" Libby said.

"Brown. Buddy Brown. Just call me Buddy."

"Buddy, we wanted to ask you some questions about when you were doing construction for the Hobson's. Are you the right Buddy who worked construction back then?" Libby moved closer to the boat.

Buddy stepped off the boat onto the pier. He took a crumpled pack of Camels out of his shirt pocket, pulled a lighter out of his pants pocket and lit a cigarette. He took a long drag and blew out the smoke.

"Yeah, I worked construction. My old man and my uncle started the company. I took over until a couple of years ago when I sold it. I'm retired."

"Do you remember doing any work on the old Hobson store on Mariposa Boulevard?" Libby asked.

He took another drag on the cigarette and blew the smoke up into the air. "That was the damnedest thing. They buy these two buildings, pay my old man to knock down a wall to make one big room, then years later, they pay us again to put the wall back up. Crazy people."

"Do you remember doing a drywall job there?" Fletcher asked.

"I've done a lot of drywall in my day. Still, do a job now and then." He took another puff and blew out the smoke. "What do you care about a forty-year-old drywall job?"

"Have you heard about the skeleton found in the wall of the old Hobson store?" Libby asked.

"What are you talking about? A dead body? In the wall?"

"Yes, sir. This young lady and the new owner were pulling down the old drywall off the south wall of the building when they found a skeleton sealed up inside the wall." Fletcher took a step forward.

Buddy turned away and took a few quick puffs of his cigarette before he flicked it into the water opposite his boat.

"I don't listen to the news much. The old Hobson store in town, you say?"

"That's right," Libby said. "Do you remember anything?"

"As I said, that's a lot of drywall jobs. But forty years ago, I was starting out working for my old man. At first, I was doing go-fer stuff, you know go for this, go for that." He laughed and ran his hands through his greasy gray hair, which made it stand up even more. "Then I learned drywall and painting. I might have done some work at that site." He paced back and forth for a few minutes, rubbing his whiskers and nodding his head. He stopped and lit another cigarette. "Come to think of it, I do remember something. I was supposed to go do the drywall at that job site, but when I went to work that day, it was already done."

"What do you mean?" Libby asked, her stomach tightening as if she'd been given a swift punch in her gut.

"Are you deaf? It was already done. When I got there to do the job, somebody else had already completed it."

"Do you know who might have done that?" Fletcher asked.

"No, and I didn't care. I was supposed to have drywalled that place the day before, but I skipped out early to go party with my friends. I came back the next day, and it was done." Buddy paced in front of the boat puffing on his cigarette, running his fingers over his face and through his hair. He suddenly stopped, his face changed, becoming one with a look of recognition or remembrance, as though a thought or a long lost memory suddenly came into view.

"What is it?" Libby asked. "Do you remember something? Do the names Melanie Cooper or Jeannette McDonald mean anything to you? What about Lynette — "

"No, I don't know those names," Buddy interrupted. "And I don't remember anything else. You've got to go." He began to shoo them, like chickens, back to the parking lot. "You all get outta here. I'm done answering your fool questions. I don't know nothing about no skeleton in a wall."

"But, Buddy…" Libby spoke to him over her shoulder. "I have a couple more names. Please."

"No buts about it, no more questions."

Buddy continued to shoo them back to the parking lot. He pushed forward and must have caught his foot on Ida's walker. He turned his ankle, hit the deck and appeared to bounce right into the water of the empty slip across from the Lilly Belle.

He came up sputtering. Fletcher leaned down to help him out of the water, but he pushed away his hands and pulled himself up onto the pier.

"Get the hell away from me," he growled. He threw his arms up and shook like a dog, throwing droplets on all of them.

"I'm so sorry, and thank you for the information." Libby continued to guide Ida back down the pier.

Ida was grumbling under her breath.

"Yes, thank you, and I'm sorry about all this," Fletcher said.

"I'll be damned. Now you got me in trouble with the harbor master." Buddy gestured toward the walkway.

An official looking man was coming towards them at a trot, but it was the next man that gave Libby pause.

"Holy Mother of God, am I in trouble now."

Detective Jack Seiler was following the harbor master down the walkway.

• • •

"You three should be glad that Mr. Brown did not press charges for assault."

They were standing in the parking lot next to Libby's SUV. Apparently, the harbor master had had enough of Buddy's shenanigans, as he called it.

Buddy said he'd stumbled and fell into the water. No problem. His visitors were leaving. He climbed into his boat, grumbling with every step.

His curse words were the only words Libby had understood during the exchange.

"Assault? It's not our fault he was drunk off his rocker." Ida straightened to her full, five-feet-eight inches.

"What are you three doing here anyway?" Jack asked, in a tone such that none of them could miss his irritation.

"Ida found Buddy's name in an old Rolodex of her husband's." Libby stood across from Jack, between Fletcher and Ida.

"I never had the heart to throw Sid's stuff away," Ida said. "I found a name under contractors and called the number." Ida explained how she got Buddy's number from the current owner.

Jack shook his head and turned to Fletcher. "Mr. Smith, I am surprised that you let these two pull you into this."

"I couldn't let them come by themselves. Besides, I had nothing better to do today." Fletcher was as calm as the glassy water of Sarasota Bay.

"He's our back-up. He has enhanced interrogation skills," Ida said.

Jack returned his gaze to Fletcher, who shrugged and smiled. "I took the course."

Turning to Libby, Jack asked, "And you, Miss Marshall. What do you have to say for yourself?"

"Well, Detective, how else are we going to find out the identity of that poor girl in the wall?"

"You need to leave this to law enforcement."

"Law enforcement? How much time are you and Sam spending on a forty-year-old cold case?" Libby pointed at Jack, her voice louder than she intended.

Jack shook his head and looked away. "There are more recent cases I need to work on."

"You know as well I that the likelihood of solving this case and getting justice for that girl and her baby is next to nothing. What else can we do?"

"He knows something," Fletcher said. "He became quite agitated, even more so when Libby mentioned those names. Though, he did seem to have quite the hangover, and three strangers showing up asking questions could make a person upset."

"What names?" Jack looked from one to the other, resting his gaze on Libby.

Libby averted her eyes.

"Names of missing persons," Ida said.

"Libby?"

"All right. I have a few names of missing persons around the time the building was empty. Buddy admitted he was on the crew that did the remodel. He said he was supposed to do the drywall, but when he went to work, the job was finished."

Jack leaned into her, basically, in effect, cornering her, as her back was now up against her SUV.

He very deliberately asked, "Where did you get these names, Libby?"

"Uh. I have a guy."

"That guy? That guy that got you intel last August?"

"Yes, that guy. The same guy that gave me valuable information that helped your case."

Jack backed away, turned to face the marina and took a breath before he turned back to continue the conversation.

"Will you share those names with me?" he asked.

"Yes, of course. I'll text them to you."

"Detective, are we free to go, or do you have other questions?" Fletcher asked.

"Yes, you can go. Just be careful, and don't get arrested. I don't want to have to bail the Three Amigos out of jail."

Libby opened the lift gate. Jack folded up the walker, and Fletcher helped Ida into the car.

"By the way, what are you doing here?" Libby asked, under her breath.

"One of those more recent cases I was telling you about. A young woman was found dead on the far side of the park early this morning." He slid the walker inside the SUV and hit the button to close the gate. "I was here to get some information from the harbor master."

"Oh my! I didn't hear anything about it. I'm sorry."

He opened the car door for her. She climbed in. He leaned into the car and said to Fletcher, "Enhanced interrogation techniques, huh?" He waved at Ida, then pointed at them, one at a time. "You three, stay out of trouble."

Before he shut the door, he whispered to Libby, "I'll see you later."

"I'm counting on that."

Chapter 13

Later that Afternoon
Accomplices

Jack strolled into the station to find Sam clearing off his desk, ready to call it a day.

Jack collapsed into his chair. "Where are you going? It's not even five o'clock."

"I have a date." Sam jiggled his keys. "Did you get anything good from the harbor master?"

"Not really." Jack laid back in his desk chair. "You know the story. Nobody saw nothing."

"Did you walk the scene?" Sam slipped his keys into his pocket.

"Yes. I think it was a body dump." Jack sat up and leaned forward onto his desk.

"I agree. Does it look familiar to you?" Sam asked.

"Yeah, that girl back in August, found out at Myakka," Jack said, referring to a nearby state park.

Sam nodded, sat back in his chair, pulled his keys out of his pocket and twirled them around on his index finger. "I was thinking the same thing. Do you think the smugglers are back in business?"

"You read my mind, partner."

Sam clenched his keys, started to get up, but then turned back to Jack. "What took you so long. I've been back from the scene for awhile." He leaned across the desk. "Did you stop at Mariposa Beach for a little afternoon delight?" Sam winked.

Jack rolled his eyes. "It gets even more interesting. You'll never guess who was at the marina."

Sam thought for a moment, then leaned back in his chair. "No. You're kidding. Libby?"

Jack nodded and ran his hands through his hair.

Sam leaned back in his chair and laughed. "That girl turns up in the most unlikely places."

"She wasn't alone this time. She had company."

Sam leaned forward. "Who was with her?"

"Ida Sullivan and Fletcher Smith."

"What were they doing there?" Sam was obviously enjoying this.

"Ida had a lead on the skeleton in the wall."

"Ida, the older woman who lives across the street from Libby? The one with the yappy dog?"

"Yes. They were talking to an old guy who lives on a boat at the marina. They were questioning him, and somehow, he ended up in the drink."

Sam leaned back and let out a roaring laugh. "This just gets better and better."

"It's not that funny." Jack's phone signaled the arrival of a text message.

Sam wiped his eyes. "What 'cha got there?"

Jack read the messages and picked up a pen and scribbled the names on a notepad. "Libby has four possible IDs for the remains in the wall."

"No way?" Sam leaned back over the desk. "Where did she get them?"

"She has a guy."

"Are you jealous?"

"No. It's a guy she used to work with back in Ohio. He must be some kind of hacker or something because she won't tell me who he is."

"Where's that list we ran?" Sam asked. "We were looking at it the other day. There were at least twenty, thirty names on that list." He came around the desk and started going through the papers in a tray on Jack's desk. "Here it is." He held up a list of names.

"Here's Libby's list. The first one is Jeanette McDonald. Ft. Myers."

Sam sat on the edge of Jack's desk and ran his finger down the list. "On the list."

"Melanie Cooper from LaBelle."

"She's on here."

Jack read the remaining two names – Lynette Watkins from Tampa and Georgia Nielsen from Venice.

"They are all on the list." Sam dropped the paper on the desk. "She has someone who can run the analysis to narrow it down and eliminate the ones that don't fit. Wow!"

"Yes, she does."

"And she won't share?"

"No."

"You should have arrested her and kept her in jail until she gives up his name."

"I thought I was going to have to arrest all three of them." Jack laughed. "Ida looked like she was going to run me over with her walker. That's probably how that old guy ended up taking a bath."

"You have your hands full with that girl and her accomplices," Sam said, shaking his head.

"She's obsessed with finding out the identity of the girl in the wall. She wants justice for that girl and her baby."

"I hope one of these leads works out," Sam said. "But I gotta go. I have dinner plans."

"Are you going out with what's her name that works in dispatch?"

"I'm having dinner with Donna." His keys were in his hands again.

"Donna? As in your ex-wife Donna?"

"Yeah." He twirled his keys. "You think that's a bad idea?"

Jack threw up his hands. "She broke your heart and stomped on it. What do you think?"

Sam flipped his keys and turned to go. He stopped and said over his shoulder, "You're probably right."

Jack watched Sam's back as he wound through the cubicles, tossing his keys in the air and catching them as he ambled to the exit.

Chapter 14

Saturday Morning
Shame, Embarrassment, and Guilt

Holiday shopping had picked up and, as a result, the café was exceptionally busy this Saturday morning, a couple of weeks before Christmas.

Mimi attributed the added business to the opening of The Mariposa Mystic, the discovery of the skeleton in the wall and the newspaper article hinting at the possibility that the new gallery could be haunted. Whatever the reason, locals and tourists were making their way to Mariposa Beach to shop in the village, have lunch at the café and end the day with drinks at The Veranda Bar at the Inn.

Mimi and Louisa were hard at work in the kitchen, while Lisa and Libby worked the front of the café.

Libby was packing a box of holiday cookies when Lisa leaned in and said, "That older guy over by the window would like to speak to you when you have a minute."

Libby surveyed the front of the café. Considering the demographics of southwest Florida, 'that older guy' was a fairly broad description of a good portion of the male population. Her eyes rested on a cleaned-up version of Buddy Brown eating a piece of pumpkin pie.

Libby closed the box, collected payment and thanked the customer. She wiped her hands on her apron, took a deep breath and picked up the coffee pot.

"Can I refill that for you, Mr. Brown?" she asked.

"Yes. Call me Buddy." He gestured toward his cup. As she filled it, he asked, "Do you have time to sit and talk for a few minutes?"

"Yes, for a bit. We've been super-busy today with holiday shoppers." Libby pulled out the chair and sat across from him.

He finished the last bite of pie and glanced up at her. "That's really good pie."

"Thanks. I'll tell Mimi." She crossed her arms on the table and waited.

Buddy wiped his mouth on his napkin, laid it on his plate, took a sip of coffee and finally, his rheumy brown eyes met her gaze. "You girls have done a really good job of fixing up this place. Are those pieces of wood part of the old bar?"

"Yes, we found them in the attic, and when we remodeled, we wanted to use what we could salvage."

"That's a pretty piece of wood." He shook his head and smiled. "We had us some good times in this place back when it was a bar. I got thrown out that side door once." He pointed at the door to the courtyard and laughed.

"We've heard some of the stories. This must have been the hot place in town."

"Yes, ma'am. It was that." He grew quiet, then said, "I reckon you're wondering what I'm doing here after what happened the other day."

Libby nodded. "You do look much better today, Buddy."

"First of all, I want to apologize for my behavior." He shook his head but wouldn't look at her. "I had had a bit too much of the hair of the dog that morning. If you know what I mean."

"I do, first hand."

He gave her a sideways glance. "I'm not sure if I believe that."

She smiled. "A story for another day. I'm sure you didn't come here to talk about hangover remedies."

"None of 'em seem to work anyways." He shuffled around in his seat. "I don't know who finished my drywall job that day. But the names of those girls did sound familiar."

She waited, arms crossed in front of her.

He blew out a breath, glanced around the room and spoke under his breath. "Jeanette McDonald worked at the Mariposa Inn for awhile back in the late seventies. We dated a bit back in the day. But as far as I know, she's alive."

"Why is she still listed as missing?"

"She got into a little trouble, so she ran away before the cops arrested her. She changed her name and started over some place else. She lives off the grid."

"Okay." Libby knew a little bit about starting over with a new name and a new life. "You said both names. What about Melanie Cooper."

"There was a guy, a painter, who worked for my dad on and off for a lot of years. His family owned a tomato farm out in LaBelle. In the off season, he'd come and work for us. When the tomatoes came in, he went home and helped with the harvest."

Libby's outward appearance remained calm, but her heart rate quickened. *Ray Ban's information said that Melanie Cooper was from LaBelle. Could this be the same family?*

"He had a younger sister who came with him one year. Pretty girl. Blonde headed, big blue eyes. A real looker."

"Did you date her, too?" Libby hoped to steer him in another direction and not go down the rabbit hole of how attractive she was.

He cackled. "No. She was too good for me. She had her sights set much higher."

"What did she do here?"

"She got a job at Hobson's supermarket out by the highway. She also worked for the catering company that was part of the market. I know that because she would come by the work site to see her brother in between jobs. I remember she wore a uniform with an apron." Buddy stopped to take a drink of coffee. Then he continued. "Coop, that's what we called her brother."

"What was his first name?" Libby wondered if he was still alive.

"I can't remember. We just called him 'Coop.' Anyways, Coop got real worried about his sister because he thought she had gotten involved with old man Hobson. Now, he was real flashy and had a reputation with the women."

"I've heard about Hobson's behavior from Ida. What did Coop think about Hobson carrying on with his sister?"

"He didn't like it much, as you can imagine. Coop said he went to see Hobson to tell him to leave his sister alone. He had a gun. He said they struggled, and the gun went off."

"Was anyone hurt?"

"No, but he was real scared that Hobson was going to have him arrested for trespassing, battery, attempted murder, whatever he could get to stick. Coop picked up his tools and headed back to LaBelle straight away. Never heard from him again, but not too long after that, I remember his sister went missing. I don't blame him for skedaddlin' out of town. There were rumors that Hobson could make a man disappear if he wanted them gone bad enough."

"Tell me, Buddy," Libby leaned in and said, "do you remember if this happened before or after Hobson's daughter disappeared?"

"It was after. I remember Hobson's daughter, another looker, by the way, went missing just around Christmastime. Melanie was later, maybe February or March. I'm not sure. Annaliese and me were in the same class in school. Only she didn't graduate that year. She was gone before Christmas."

Chapter 15

Saturday Evening
The Boat Parade

Libby pulled into the circular, bricked driveway of the Bird Key address that Jack had given her.

"Holy Mother of God," she muttered aloud as she took in the view.

A two-story stucco mansion of, what appeared to Libby to be Italian design, stood in front of her. She stopped and gazed at the portico and the second level balcony. *No way…is that a veranda?*

Jack told her to follow the driveway around the side to the guest house. Reluctantly pulling her eyes away from the front entrance, she slowly followed the driveway around the side where the view exploded with light reflecting off the water of the intracoastal waterway which ran between the mainland, Bird Key and the barrier islands.

He was standing on the porch of a small cottage to the left of where she stopped her SUV.

He opened her car door and asked, "What do you think of my little place?"

"What are you doing? There's no way a cop can afford to live in a place like this." Libby walked toward the water. "This is beautiful."

"It is beautiful. I'm basically housesitting, a glorified pool boy."

"Are your friends, for whom you're a glorified pool boy and free security guard, ever here?"

"Yes, they're usually here by now, but they're spending Christmas and New Years in New York with family."

He slipped his arms around her waist and she leaned back onto his shoulder.

"And all you did was solve their robbery case and get their stuff back?"

He kissed her neck and laughed. "Most of it." He spun her around so that she was facing him and gave her a proper welcoming kiss. "Come in. I have some food for us before we walk across the street to the park."

• • •

Jack had laid out an antipasto with wine and cheese on the kitchen table. He poured her a glass of red wine and offered her a seat on the porch.

"This is fabulous. I'm impressed."

"Thanks." He tapped her wine glass with his. "Thank goodness, the market is on my way home."

Libby sat back in her chair, sipped her wine and enjoyed the view for a few minutes, then she asked, "Guess who came to see me today?"

"Who?" He popped a cube of cheese in his mouth.

"A very cleaned up and apologetic Buddy Brown." She spread cheese on a cracker and took a bite.

"What did he want?"

"He told me that he knew both of the names I mentioned that day at the marina." She told him what Buddy had said about Jeanette McDonald and Melanie Cooper. "I think the information we've gathered so far points to Melanie Cooper as the remains we found in the wall."

"If that's the case, I wonder where Jeanette McDonald has been for forty years?" Jack sat back in his chair and sipped his wine.

"I can't say that her story didn't strike a cord with me. Who else do you know who left home, changed her name and started a new life?" She raised her eyebrows and pulled a few grapes off the stem.

"And I am so glad she did."

• • •

The sun was beginning to set as they crossed the street and joined a growing crowd gathered at the east end of the park. Jack explained that the boats were being staged further up the key and would follow a route that would bring them directly in front of the park before sailing under the John Ringling Causeway to Marina Jacks, a local marina and restaurant, where judges would rate the boats on their decorating creativity.

"Jack, good to see you." An elderly man with a paunch and a captain's hat greeted him with a handshake and a back slap.

Jack introduced Libby to the man and his petite wife who had a clear thermos of a fruity looking drink that Libby was sure was not fruit punch.

"It's so nice to meet you, Libby." The woman shook her hand. "We were wondering if Jack had a girlfriend. He hasn't come to our dinner parties lately."

"You can always bring her along," the man said.

Libby thought his name was Harold but she wasn't sure.

"Let us know the date of the next party," Jack said. "It all depends on our schedules. The life of a cop, you know."

"We were so happy when Jack moved in," chimed in a slim woman in a pink running outfit. "He makes us feel so much more secure."

Jack led her away from the group, then whispered, "The only reason they invited me to those parties was to fix me up with the friends, daughters and granddaughters. Now that they've seen you, I hope the matchmaking will stop."

"Me, too. You might meet someone you like better than me," Libby teased.

"Not a chance." He kissed her temple.

Libby didn't know much about boats except that the yachts and the other sleek, big boats cost more than her house, Ida's house and Mimi's house put together, but she enjoyed being in the warmth of Jack's arms as they watched the festive boats sail by. The crowd cheered the boats and their crew as they sailed under the causeway.

"Hey, Jack."

Libby thought it was Harold calling him.

"Come over here. We have a boat question."

"I'll be right back." Jack kissed her ear.

At his kiss, her heart flipped. She felt like a high school girl on her first date. She smiled as she watched him in animated conversation with Harold and a group of men a few yards away.

She suddenly felt movement behind her. Thinking it was another parade-goer looking for a better view, she shifted her position. Then, she felt something sharp at her right flank.

"Don't move and don't make a sound or I will stick you good," a low raspy voice said in her ear.

She took in a quick breath, smelling beer on his breath as he poked her with a knife. "Quit sticking your nose in something that is none of your damn business. Back off. It was forty years ago. Back off, or you'll be sorry, little lady."

He gave her one last poke with the knife and was gone.

"Libby, are you all right? You are white as a ghost." Jack took her in his arms.

She was shaking and taking in air in short gasps.

"Take a deep breath."

She did as he asked, then took another and let it out slowly.

"A…a man threatened me."

"What?!" Jack looked around and held her tighter.

"He had a knife."

"Did he cut you?!" Jack ran his hands up under her shirt. "I don't feel anything, but let's go home."

He pulled a flashlight out of his pocket and, with his arm around her waist, led her across the street.

• • •

"He told me to mind my own business or I'd be sorry. I was scared to death that he would stab me in my kidney, and I would bleed out before you could get to me."

As soon as they were inside the house, Jack removed her sweater and pulled her shirt over her head.

"There's a small prick, but no real break in the skin." He rubbed her side where the man had held the point of the blade.

She held up her sweater and found a small hole. "I really like this sweater."

He gently took the sweater out of her hands and examined it. "A couple of stitches will pull the threads back together. Good as new."

"I was so scared. I could see you just a few feet away from me, but I was frozen. I couldn't do anything."

Jack pulled her into his embrace. "I hope you will heed his advice, because so far, you haven't listened to me."

"This tells me that we're onto something. Do you think…"

He kissed her on the right side of her neck.

"I think that Melanie Cooper…"

He kissed her on the left side of her neck.

"Jack."

"Hmmm?"

He kissed her nose.

"I suppose we can talk about this tomorrow," she said, slipping her arms around his neck.

Chapter 16

Mariposa Beach
The Launch Party

In the two weeks leading up to Christmas, there was lots of activity at The Devereaux Gallery.

The Monday after the Boat Parade, Steve was using the café as his office while the hardwood floors were being refinished. One of the items on his list was contracting with Mimi to cater the gallery opening. They had their heads together over the possible menu when Kenji burst in with the exciting news that he had confirmed the attendance of the New York art dealer.

A few days later, painters were busy painting the first floor. Once they were finished, The Gallery was on lockdown. No one, except Kenji, was allowed inside.

Steve stopped by the café on Christmas Eve as he was leaving to drive home to Charleston for Christmas.

"Why won't you let us see inside the gallery?" Mimi asked, standing in front of the counter, hands on her hips.

Libby laughed. "You know you're driving her crazy with all this secrecy, don't you?" She was making Steve's extra large latte for the drive.

"I don't want you to see it until it's all finished. I have a surprise for y'all."

"I bet Rachel has seen it," Mimi said.

"No, Rachel has not seen it, at least not since it was painted."

Libby handed Steve his coffee and a bag containing his favorite orange scones. "Safe travels. I'll make sure she doesn't break into the gallery while you're gone. Merry Christmas."

"Thank you. I'm going across the courtyard to see Rachel, and then I'm on the road. Merry Christmas to you both."

"Merry Christmas," Mimi said.

"I'll be back the day the after Christmas. We have an opening to do."

• • •

Christmas came and went quietly, which is exactly how Libby liked it. David had gone to New York to celebrate Christmas with friends from his Broadway days and participate in a Christmas charity show. She suspected he missed the hustle and bustle of New York City and although he enjoyed teaching, she knew he missed performing, and occasionally worried he would return there permanently.

Libby and Jack had Christmas Eve dinner with Julia at her condo. Mr. Mendelson, Julia's neighbor, joined them for a wonderful roast beef dinner.

Libby spent the night at Jack's. He presented her with a beautiful necklace, one she had been eying at Rachel's shop. Libby had done her own undercover work with Sam regarding Jack's fishing-related gift. Libby wasn't exactly sure what it was, but Jack liked it or at least acted like he did. In the end, everyone was happy, and Libby enjoyed another early morning in Jack's arms on the porch watching the new day arrive.

On Christmas Day, they were invited for dinner to Jack's sister's, where she met Jack's father, his sisters and brothers, their spouses or significant others and children. They were all very welcoming to her and seemed to be happy their brother had moved on from his divorce. His oldest sister, Beverly, confided that she never really liked Jack's wife anyway.

Their large family holiday dinner reminded Libby of her childhood holidays with her O'Brien cousins on her father's side. Good food, good cheer and kids running around playing with their toys. For Libby, this was one of the best Christmases in a long time.

• • •

Three days before the launch, Mimi noticed that Kenji's car had been parked in front of the gallery until long after the lunch rush. She pointed this out to Libby.

"I bet they're moving Kenji's art into the gallery," Mimi said.

Libby joined her at the window. "What do you think his sculptures look like?"

"Some kind of abstract work, I think." Mimi stepped closer.

The Christmas tree was situated in the middle of the two windows that met at the southeast corner. The crystal mistletoe ornament, hung in the window, created rainbows in the mid-afternoon sun. Mimi and Libby stood on opposite sides of the tree in order to get the best views.

"There must be a truck bringing the stuff in the back," Libby said.

They watched Fletcher Smith walk towards the café from the direction of the gallery. When he arrived, Mimi peppered him with questions.

"I can confirm there is a rental van pulled up to the back door, but unfortunately, I couldn't see anything." He joined them at the tree, standing on Mimi's side. "What is it with all the secrecy?"

"It's for effect," Libby said. "He want us to see it for the first time when it's all put together."

"He says he has a surprise." Mimi turned to Fletcher. "Can I get you something?"

"Not really, I was taking my afternoon walk, when I saw you two gazing out the window like a couple of puppies. I wondered what was going on, but since I'm here, I'll have a cup of coffee and some pumpkin pie."

• • •

Right on schedule at three o'clock on New Year's Eve, Libby backed her SUV up to the rear door of the gallery and hit the button to activate the lift gate. She and Mimi had prepped the hors d'oeuvres and baked the desserts the day before, then put them together New Year's Eve morning. They went home to change, then Libby returned to the café and packed the food into her car. Mimi was going to meet her at the gallery.

"I love your dress," Mimi said, arriving at the gallery just behind Libby. "It's so nice that your aunt owns a store."

"Thanks. You should have seen the short, black, sequined number she had picked out for me. It would have been great if all I had to do was stand around and glitter." Libby had opted for a longer, less form-fitting, maroon dress with black beading. It had a low, flattering neckline and capped sleeves. "Your dress is very pretty, too."

Mimi wore a dress with a black, fitted bodice with a v-neckline and black and gold, flared skirt.

Steve appeared wearing a black suit with an open-collared, white shirt. "I've got the table all set up."

"Wow, you look very nice," Libby said.

Mimi nodded in agreement.

"My mama taught me to clean up well. By the way, besides making fabulous food, I think I have the best looking caterers on the whole west coast of Florida."

He picked up a tray and carried it inside. They laughed and followed.

A table was set up near the back door. Mimi brought in a black tablecloth and carried a centerpiece of Christmas greens with white and red poinsettias. Steve had saved Eleanor's elegant, flower-patterned china, a Christmas set as well as a white china set. They used the salad plates for the table. Mimi made a sparkling punch. White and red wine were available as well as water and iced tea.

After they completed the set up, they stood back and admired their work.

"You ladies have outdone yourselves. It looks fabulous," Steve said, giving them each a hug.

Libby gestured around her. "What looks fabulous is this gallery."

Mimi was examining a beautiful, multi-hued glass orb with what appeared to have tentacles materializing from within its core. "Did Kenji do this?"

"Yes, he did," Steve said. "And that bowl over there and the obelisk on the pedestal in the corner."

"This glass work is amazing," Mimi said.

"What is this?" Libby asked. She was standing in front of the exposed brick wall, now cleaned and shiny, all of the grime and drywall dust long removed. In the middle of the wall, a white sheet covered a large object.

Mimi joined her in front of the wall. "It looks like a painting."

"Are you going to unveil it tonight?" Libby asked. "How about a sneak peek?"

"I'm waiting on Rachel. I want to show it to all three of you at the same time. But I will unveil it before the opening starts."

Mimi checked her watch. "She'd better hurry up. It's three forty-five."

All three turned at a knock on the back door. They were disappointed when it turned out to be Paul, Mimi's husband. He had stayed home to wait on the babysitter.

"Did I forget something?" he asked in response to their stares.

"No, Paul," Libby said. "We thought you were Rachel."

Paul joined them in front of the painting.

"Honey, when Rachel gets here, Steve's going to give us a sneak preview of this painting."

"Who's the artist?" Paul asked.

"I am," Steve said. "I painted this especially for the opening."

"Is that why we haven't seen much of you these last weeks?" Libby asked.

"Other than getting this place in shape, I've been spending my mornings on this work."

Paul wandered over to the food table to examine what his wife had prepared. He reached for a stuffed mushroom, but before he could pick it up, Mimi smacked his hand away, telling him to wait until the other guests arrive.

Rachel rushed through the door a few minutes later, apologetic for being a bit late.

"Okay. Rachel's here," Mimi said. "Pull off the sheet before anyone else gets here."

Steve took both of Rachel's hands in his and said, "Rachel, I want you to be the one to remove the sheet. It was you who gave me the inspiration and the vision."

Libby and Mimi exchanged glances. Rachel's eyes were only on Steve's.

"All right." She dropped his hands and stood in front of the painting. "Wow, this seems like an honor."

She moved to the side of the painting and gingerly grasped the side of the sheet.

"Is this like christening a ship?" Mimi asked.

Steve nodded. "I guess it's the same type of honor."

"Go ahead. What are you waiting on?" Libby asked, her voice edgy with anticipation.

Rachel slowly pulled on the edge of the sheet. It fell in slow motion. Libby thought it was never going to slide off the side of the painting.

When it finally fell to the floor, a starkly white painting of a young woman with white blonde hair falling in waves over her shoulders was revealed. A white dove in flight carried a green twig in its mouth. The woman wore a flowing, white, empire gown, her right hand reaching out toward the dove, the other cupping a small baby bump. Her crystal blue eyes were the most outstanding element of the portrait.

Libby could not turn away from the expressive eyes that seemed to bore into her.

"Steve, this is the most beautiful portrait I've ever seen," Libby said. "How did you get this image?"

"From the way Rachel described her the day we did the smudge."

Rachel was still standing next to the painting, tears streaming down her face. "That's her." She turned to Steve. "You saw her through me. It's her." She fell into Steve's arms.

"Who is that girl?" Paul asked.

Mimi picked a cocktail napkin from the top of a stack on the adjacent drink table and wiped a tear. "It's the girl in the wall."

"I thought they didn't know who she was."

Mimi sniffed. "They don't."

Paul scratched his head. "If they don't know who it is, how did he paint her portrait?"

"Rachel saw her in a vision."

"What?"

"Why don't you get some punch. It might make more sense if you drink a little."

Kenji flew in the back door. "What's going on? The front door is still locked." He unlocked the front door and flung it open.

"No one is here but us," Steve said.

"We need to be ready." Kenji went to the drink table and poured himself a glass of white wine. He surveyed the group. "You all look very nice. This is going to be a successful, fabulous, perfect evening."

Libby wasn't sure if he was trying to convince them or himself.

Kenji stopped in front of the portrait. "Is that what you've been working on?"

"Yes. It's called *Peace and Forgiveness*."

"What a beautiful name," Rachel said through her tears.

Rachel and Steve embraced again.

Mimi leaned in and whispered to Libby, "What is going on with those two?"

"Maybe one of your matchmaking schemes actually worked out?"

"Hello." They turned to see a young lady at the front door. "Where should I set up my harp?"

• • •

Twenty minutes later, the gallery was full, and the room filled with melodious harp music. Kenji and Steve were beaming with pride in their work. In addition to the new painting, Steve also had multiple photographs and other paintings and sketches. Libby was impressed with the quality of the work they promoted.

The men from The Company arrived at almost the same time. Mr. Strauss arrived last with Brigitte in tow. They stopped by the drink table then convened in front of the portrait with the other men. Brigitte shook her head and moved on to examine the obelisk in the corner. She was a small, wiry woman, her short, light hair slicked back accentuating her face's sharp edges.

Libby was minding the drink table when she caught a glimpse of Jack at the door. He came in with Ellen Sanders and another woman. Ellen's tight bun was gone, and her hair fell in waves over her shoulders.

Libby waved at Jack across the room, and he made his way to her side, stopping to shake Steve's hand and congratulate him on the launch.

Jack kissed her and accepted a glass of wine. "Wow, there's a lot of people here."

"See that guy talking to Kenji?"

Jack nodded.

"That's the New York art dealer. This could be huge for them."

"By the way, you look absolutely gorgeous tonight," Jack said, kissing her again.

"Thanks. I'll tell Julia you approve."

He sipped his wine, then leaned in to whisper, "I do have a couple of things to tell you tonight."

"Oh yeah?"

She poured wine into a glass and handed it to a woman in a skin tight red dress. Libby saw her arrive with the art dealer.

"I have information on Jeanette McDonald and the guy who threatened you at the park."

Libby set the wine bottle on the table. "Let's go out back."

Jack brought his glass and followed her out the back door.

Once outside, he said, "After that little incident at the Boat Parade, I decided to dig deeper into Jeanette because of what Buddy told you about her being alive and living off the grid. I started doing a few searches, calling on a few friends. She works in a bait shop. She got married, changed her name and goes by Janet."

"So, you know where she is?"

"I do. She lives in Everglades City. I have a cousin who lives down there. He checked her out for me. Buddy must have put the word out. I think it was her husband who held you at knife point. He wanted to scare you off, but I don't think he meant to hurt you."

Libby walked about the parking lot with her hand over her mouth. "He accomplished that all right. What are you going to do now?"

"I'd like to get a warrant to arrest him for assault with a deadly weapon, but I have no real proof it was him who threatened you."

"You're right. I didn't see him. I wasn't hurt…just scared."

"That scared the life out of me!" He stopped, blew out a breath, regaining control. "Libby, he held a knife to your back and threatened to kill you."

"I know, but it's Christmas, and I wasn't hurt. Just let it go for now. Please."

"All right. For now, but I'm going to keep checking into him, and if I get one shred of proof, I'm getting that warrant."

"Thank you." She kissed him. "We'd better go back in. I'm shirking my beverage duties."

He shook his head and kissed her again, then opened the door.

She was halfway inside when she turned and said, "Did you see the portrait of the woman in white on the wall?"

Jack shook his head. "No."

"You need to."

• • •

Back inside, Libby helped Mimi replenish the food while Jack walked around. He stopped in front of the portrait on the wall. He read the title plate and turned to catch Libby's gaze across the room. She smiled and nodded. He turned back to the portrait as a woman bumped into his elbow.

"Excuse me," she said.

"That's all right." He glanced at her, back at the portrait, then immediately returned his gaze to her. "You look familiar. Do I know you?"

She was a small woman, only about five feet tall, late fifties or early sixties, gray hair cut in a short bob."

She looked him up and down. "You look familiar, too." She pointed at him. "Are you Bobby Seiler's youngest boy?"

"Yes, ma'am, I am." He thought for a minute, then turned back to her. "Are you Mrs. Petersen, the vet's wife?"

"Bingo."

"Oh, I'm sorry. I think I remember my father telling me Doc Petersen passed recently and your son has taken over the practice."

She nodded. "Yes, he did. It's all good."

"Arcadia is a long way to come for something like this."

"What…are you a cop?" she asked.

"Yes, actually." He offered his hand. "Detective Jack Seiler at your service."

She shook his hand. "Your daddy must be so proud. I haven't seen him in years."

"Yes, ma'am."

She continued staring at the portrait. "I used to live around here. I was visiting my daughter in Englewood and saw the story in the paper. I thought I'd come check it out."

"I remember your husband coming out to the ranch. I used to tag along behind him, my dad and older brothers out to the barn." Jack looked around. "How rude of me. Can I get you something to drink?"

"No, thank you. I have to go. I just wanted to stop in real quick. My curiosity got the best of me."

"Attention, everyone." Steve was clanging a fork against a wine glass. "Thank you all for being here. Kenji and I are so excited at the turn out. Enjoy our exhibition and have some more of the delicious food from the Mariposa Café. Good night."

Jack turned his attention back to the woman.

"It was good to see you." She took one last glance at the portrait. "I must go."

"I will tell my dad I saw you."

"Please do." She turned towards the door and then back to Jack. "I always wondered what happened to that gold digger Melanie Cooper."

She continued to the front door.

The lights flickered for a second.

She looked up, then back at Jack and winked.

A thought crossed his mind. *Could that be? No, it couldn't be, could it?*

Libby appeared at his elbow. "Jack, who was that woman? You look like you've seen a ghost or something."

"You wouldn't believe me if I told you."

Chapter 17

Happy New Year

"Do you think that woman was her?" Libby asked.

They had returned to Libby's house from the New Year's Eve party at the Mariposa Inn. She hugged herself, taking in his scent before she slipped off his jacket and laid it gently across a chair. It was a chilly evening. On the walk home, he had helped her into his coat to ward off the cold and stop her shivering.

It was a fun evening that had continued from the gallery opening to the party at the Mariposa Inn where they had dinner with dancing afterwards. They celebrated Steve's successful gallery opening, Rachel's new shop, and they toasted to continuous success for the café and the new businesses. David and Ben played their favorite tunes, and Libby even joined them for a few.

"I do think it was her." Jack loosened his tie and removed a glass from the cupboard and filled it with water from the tap. "I called my dad to wish him Happy New Year, and I asked him about her."

"What did he say?" Libby leaned across the counter.

All evening she had wondered who the mysterious woman was who had appeared at the gallery opening. Her eyes barely left the portrait of the girl in white.

"He said that The Petersens were both in the circus before Mr. Petersen became a veterinarian. Annie used to work the horses. My dad remembered Annie telling him about riding in the same trailer with the horses between circus performances."

"Annie?"

"Yes. Her name is Annie Petersen."

"Jack, does this mean that Annie Petersen is Annaliese Hobson? Annie could be a nickname for Annaliese. She's been hiding in plain sight all these years."

"I think so."

Jack took his water glass into the living room. Libby followed, slipping off her shoes after she plopped onto the sofa.

"It's amazing that she's been able to stay hidden so long. Her and Jeanette McDonald."

"Not really. You've done it."

He sat next to her on the sofa and placed his water glass on the small coffee table.

"Touché." She shook her head, hesitated for a moment, and then said," I can't help realizing the similarities between the three of us – Annaliese Hobson, Jeanette McDonald and me. All three of us left everything behind and started over with new names, new lives."

"Each of you had some kind of event that pushed you toward that decision."

"That's true – Annie Hobson Petersen had an abusive father, Jeanette committed a crime and was running from the law, and then there's me, betrayed, wounded…and hurt. All of us on the run."

"But, as you said, each of you have made new lives, good lives." Jack ran his forefinger along her cheek. "You've become quite introspective tonight."

"It's a new year. So much can change from one year to the next. Look at us. We didn't even know each other last New Year's."

Jack gave a little snort. "Last New Year's Eve, I was on-call, and I never would have believed this New Year's would be any different. But, here we are."

She met his gaze and asked, "What are you going to do about Annie?"

When he didn't answer right away, she laid her head back on the sofa and stretched.

"Nothing." He shrugged. "She hasn't committed any crime."

"You're right. There's no crime in joining the circus and then moving to Arcadia."

Jack grew quiet, then turned to Libby, took her hand and ran his fingers across her knuckles "Libby, I need to tell you something."

"That sounds ominous." Her smile faded, and she pulled her hand away.

He turned to face her, his arm stretched across the back of the sofa, close enough for him to touch her shoulder.

"It's nothing bad," he said.

He settled into the sofa and began to make small circles on her bare shoulder.

Her red hair was pulled into an up-do with tendrils falling about her face and down her back. The soft light bounced off the shiny black beads on her dress.

"You are so beautiful," he said.

"Thanks. You look pretty dapper yourself."

She leaned in and kissed him. She pulled back, but he embraced her into an even deeper kiss.

She finally backed away and asked, "This is very nice, but what did you want to tell me before we got side tracked? I don't like things hanging over my head. Just pull the band-aid off."

He chuckled, kissed her lightly on the forehead and then rested his forehead against hers. "I do need to tell you this."

He sat back, just out of her reach. "It appears that the trafficking ring has started up again."

She pulled her feet under her on the sofa. "The girl at the marina?"

"Yes, the circumstances are very much like the girl we found out by Myakka last August. Do you remember?"

The previous August, Libby's friend Pilar was kidnapped after she discovered a money laundering scheme at her place of employment. Libby was called to the morgue to make a possible identification. It was not Pilar, and the girl remained a Jane Doe.

"Yes," Libby smiled. "I call that our first date."

"The county morgue? I would say the conversation at the restaurant afterwards was more like a first date."

She smiled at the teasing.

"Do you know if it's the same players as last time?" Libby unconsciously massaged the scar in the palm of her right hand.

"I don't know, but there are similarities in the way they're running this operation."

"The information on the missing flash drive must have been de-coded," Libby said.

In the confusion of the rescue operation in Key West, a flash drive containing in-depth accounting, distribution and location information was never found. Libby had her suspicions of what happened to it, but she was never able to prove it.

"It appears so."

"What about Max Holden?" she asked. "Is he still in Witness Protection?"

"As far as I know," Jack said. "But if you ever hear from him, you must report it."

"Of course, but I don't think he would break protection and come around here," she said. "I would think this would be the last place he would show up. There are cops here all the time."

She playfully stroked his cheek.

"He sent you that song, so he obviously has some fascination or connection with you."

Before Holden went into Witness Protection, he sent Libby a song he had written as a gift.

"He can have it back. It creeps me out." Libby shuddered. "David still has it."

"Good."

"Is that all you needed to tell me?" she asked, her hand on his thigh.

He ran his fingers up her right cheek and into her hair. He slowly pulled on the pearled comb that held that side of her updo. "No, it isn't."

Her hair loosened but didn't fall.

"Okay," she said, removing her hand from his thigh.

"The Florida Department of Law Enforcement has created a new task force that will involve several local agencies up and down the west coast from St. Petersburg to Naples."

"And they've asked you to participate?"

He slipped the comb from the left side out of her hair. The curls tumbled to her shoulders.

"Yes," he said. "It will be in addition to my current case load, and it will probably involve surveillance and undercover work."

She shook her curls loose, watching him as she did so.

"This is a good thing for your career," she said. "I know that."

He twirled his finger around an errant curl. "It is."

"My mother hated it when my dad went undercover, and the few times I went undercover, I never told her." She leaned forward. "I remember that rush of adrenalin, that high you get with fear and excitement. I know my dad had it, and I know you have it, too."

"It's important to me that you understand." He took her hand, running his thumb across hers. "A lot of women would not."

"Are you talking about your ex-wife?" she asked.

"Yes, but let's not." He pulled her to him. "That's in the past."

He kissed her, his hands in her hair.

"Happy New Year," she said and kissed him back. "I'm glad we're beginning it together. And I'm looking forward to a very good year."

Mariposa Café Recipes

Grandma Grace's Chocolate Meringue Pie

A holiday staple especially on Christmas Eve

¾ cup sugar
3-4 tablespoons Hershey's (or your favorite) cocoa*
3 tablespoons cornstarch
Dash of salt
2 cups of milk
3 eggs, separated
2 tablespoons (1/4 stick) butter
1 teaspoon vanilla
1 baked 9 inch pie shell
½ teaspoon cream of tartar
¼ cup plus 2 tablespoons sugar

Combine the ¾ cup sugar, cornstarch, cocoa, and salt in the top of a double boiler** Mix well. Add about 2 inches of water in the bottom of the double boiler.

Combine the milk and egg yolks in a separate bowl. Beat with a wire whisk until frothy, about 1 to 2 minutes.

Gradually stir the milk and eggs into the sugar mixture, mixing well.

Cook over medium heat, stirring constantly until the mixture is thickened to a pudding consistency. The water in the bottom of the double boiler will be bubbly.

Remove from heat. Add the butter and vanilla. Stir until the butter is melted and the pie filling is smooth.

Spoon into the baked pie crust shell.

Meringue:

Using an electric mixer, beat the egg whites (at room temperature) and cream of tartar at the highest mixer speed. Gradually add the ¼ cup plus 2 tablespoons sugar, beating until stiff peaks form and the sugar is fully dissolved.

Spread meringue over the hot filling, sealing to the edge of the pastry. Bake at 350 degrees for 10-12 minutes or until gold brown.

*If you use unsweetened chocolate, increase the sugar by ¼ cup.

** If you don't have a double boiler, you can improvise by using two saucepans or one saucepan and a metal mixing bowl as long as the bowl doesn't touch the water in the bottom pan. The top pan should seal off the lower pan to hold in the steam in order to cook the food in the top pan/bowl.

A Note From the Author

Thank you for reading *Mistletoe and Missing Persons*, my first Mariposa Café short holiday mystery. I hope you enjoyed the latest adventure with Libby, Mimi, Jack, and the other fun and quirky characters in Mariposa Beach as much as I have enjoyed expanding their little world.

If you enjoyed the book, please consider writing a review on Amazon or Goodreads, even if it's just a sentence or two. Word-of-mouth is the best way for authors to grow readership and for other readers to find my books. Your reviews are important and are so appreciated. If you give the recipes that I include in my books a try, let me know how you like them. The chocolate pie recipe included at the end of this story is an old family holiday favorite.

You can connect with me:

Facebook at Teresa Michael – Author
Instagram at @teresamichael1

Happy reading. I'm busy working on Libby's future adventures and perhaps begin a few other projects as well.

Teresa Michael
November 2019

Acknowledgements

Thank you to the Inkylinks Writers Group – Jim, Lizzie, Marisa, Pam, Rob, Shirley, and Teri. Thanks for listening, encouragement, and helping to work out the kinks. I love our little group.

To my beta readers on this story – Pam Menard, Sheila Smith, and Judy Timmons. Thanks for your great comments and input.

Continued thanks to the Sarasota Ex Libris Book Club for their continued expansion of my reading horizons and for their support and friendship over the years.

Thanks to Anne Mahalik for Devereaux.

Thanks to Sheila Smith for the smudge lesson and your love and friendship.

Thanks to Sunny Birdsong for sharing your stories about working the horses and traveling with the circus. I truly enjoyed hearing them.

Thank you to Dee Dee Scott at Let Love Glow Author Services for the wonderful editing, encouragement, and keeping me on track along this authorpreneur publishing journey.

To those who read the first Mariposa book, I appreciate all the great reviews and feedback. You all have made my year with all the positive responses I've received. Thank you from the bottom of my heart. I hope you enjoy this one as well.

Last but certainly not least - Thanks to Larry for his support, first draft editing, building and construction consultations, honest feedback and love.

About the Author

Teresa Michael's professional career is in health information management and technology and she is currently the Director of Health Information Management at a large health care system in Florida. She returned to college in her fifties, and instead of following the healthcare informatics path, she followed her passion and earned a degree in Creative Writing from Eckerd College in St. Petersburg, FL.

Teresa has always loved a good mystery and has turned her love of writing and mystery stories into her first mystery novel. She likes to read and belongs to a book club whose members have pushed her out of her comfort zone into enjoying all genres, though a good mystery is still her first choice.

She loves to travel and has visited forty-nine states having spent nine years on the road working *for a healthcare software vendor. She also spent many years as the Team Manager of the U.S. Archery team for the 1996 Olympic Games in Atlanta, Georgia and the 2000 Olympic Games in Sydney, Australia as well as other international tournaments all over the world.

She lives in Sarasota, Florida with her husband and two cats, Lily and Lido. She enjoys visiting her children and grandchildren and loves spending time with her family creating new memories. She's busy working on the next Mariposa Café mystery and planning her next trip, hopefully to that fiftieth state.

Books by Teresa Michael

Mariposa Café Mysteries
Murder in Mariposa Beach
Mistletoe and Missing Persons (A Mariposa Café Short
Holiday Mystery)
Deception in Mariposa Beach --- *Coming Soon!*

Short Fiction
Indian Rock